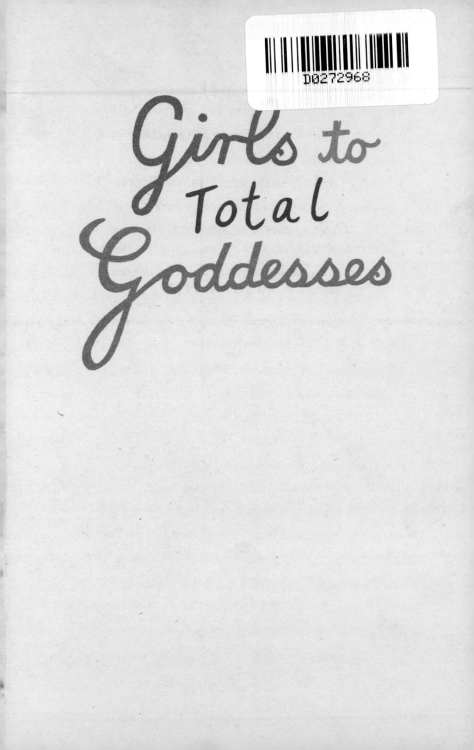

Girls to Total Goddesses

Also by Sue Limb

Girl, 15: Flirting for England
Girl, 15: Charming But Insane
Girl, (Nearly) 16: Absolute Torture
Girl, 16: Pants on Fire
Girls, Guilty But Somehow Glorious
(Previously published as *Zoe and Chloe: On the Prowl*)
Girls, Muddy, Moody Yet Magnificent
(Previously published as *Zoe and Chloe: Out to Lunch*)

Girls
to
Total
Goddesses

SUE
LIMB

BLOOMSBURY

LONDON BERLIN NEW YORK SYDNEY

Bloomsbury Publishing, London, Berlin and New York

First published in Great Britain in 2009 by Bloomsbury Publishing Plc
36 Soho Square, London, W1D 3QY

A CIP catalogue record of this book is available from the British Library

ISBN 978 0 7475 8274 8

FSC
Mixed Sources
Product group from well-managed
forests and other controlled sources
Cert no. SGS - COC - 2061
www.fsc.org
© 1996 Forest Stewardship Council

Typeset by Dorchester Typesetting Group Ltd
Printed in Great Britain by Clays Ltd, St Ives plc

3 5 7 9 10 8 6 4 2

www.bloomsbury.com/childrens
www.suelimbbooks.co.uk

For Anna Wednesday Meyers

Chapter 1

'Right,' said Chloe. 'When are we going to start our makeovers and transform ourselves into goddesses?' We were snuggling in the warmth of the Dolphin Cafe, one foggy afternoon in November. We'd been busy with school stuff for weeks, so we'd had to put the goddess project on hold. Further delay could prove disastrous, however: I felt we were beginning to drift.

'Right now!' I insisted. 'We've got to get started! Remember what we said back in the summer? Girls to goddesses in seven days. Anyway, I have to be irresistible by eight o'clock tonight.'

'Eight o'clock? What's happening at eight o'clock? You never mentioned anything.' Chloe's eyes widened excitedly.

'Who knows?' I smiled mysteriously. 'Once we're goddesses, the sky's the limit!' I had slightly randomly fixed on eight o'clock as a time for our new lives to begin. Eight sounds so much more major and exciting than seven, come to think of it. Maybe it should be girls to goddesses in eight days: we might need an extra day to complete our transformation.

'So where do we start?' Chloe whipped out her notebook and wrote the words *GODDESS PROJECT* at the top of a page.

'Well,' I mused, staring into the muddy remains of my hot chocolate, 'I've got to transform myself. I mean, you're amazing, you're totally cool and stuff, but I'm just hideous from head to toe! My hair's like wire, my nose is a turnip, my teeth are too big, I have the largest spot in the history of acne . . .' (Nigel, incidentally – he's such a big presence in my life, he's become more of a pet than a blemish) '. . . my tum is like an air bag, my legs are fat, I'm knock-kneed and pigeon-toed . . . I come flubbering out of bed in the morning like a Thing from the Bottom of the Sea, all slime and tentacles.'

'Stop! Stop!' laughed Chloe. 'Zoe, don't be stupid! You're gorgeous! You've got an hourglass figure to die for, your hair is crinkly and all glittery and bronzy, your eyelashes are huge, your legs are endless, you're tall and commanding and amazing and funny. I'm the one who needs a transformation!'

'No!' I protested. 'That's rubbish!'

'Listen!' insisted Chloe. 'I'm basically a dwarf, I have no boobs – they're smaller than your average walnuts, my hair is dry and demented and worst of all horribly, horribly RED and clashes with everything, my skin is the colour of porridge and covered with horrendous freckles, so I look like a goddam TOAD, plus the moment I go into the sun I get barbecued – oh, and my legs! Hideous and stringy! My shinbones are so sharp, you could cut cheese with them! Nobody is ever going to want to marry me!'

'Yes, they are!' I told her. 'You're a perfect petite size 8, for God's sake! Your hair is a divine red cloud! Your skin is like flawless snow and totally without polar bears' footprints! Next time they make a film about Queen Elizabeth I, Cate Blanchett will be out of a job!'

At this point Maria, who owns the cafe, came up and asked us to keep the noise down. 'You're disturbing other customers,' she hissed in a surly manner. Although she is basically a tyrant obsessed with men, we have to keep on the right side of her because the Dolphin Cafe is the place to be. Our mate Toby was a waiter here back in the summer hols, and he told us that Maria let him kiss her in the pantry on Thursdays.

'So where do we start?' whispered Chloe.

'It's got to be exercise,' I said determinedly. 'Because I can't give up on food. Not yet. And apparently exercise improves brain function, too.'

'Yes! Yes!' Chloe nodded, writing down *EXCERSISE*. Her spelling's not brilliant, but she can do amazing sums in her head. 'Exercise is a great idea! Maybe I can find an exercise to develop my boobs! And our skin will glow and our eyes will sparkle . . .'

'With supernatural fire!' I agreed. 'But I'm not going to exercise *in public*. I don't want anyone to see my flab flapping.'

'Yeah!' Chloe shuddered. 'That would be weird!' It certainly would be weird if Chloe's flab flapped, because she basically has about as much cellulite as a pixie. 'Also I don't want anything to do with ball games!' she added. Chloe's wonderfully unco-ordinated in a hilarious kind of way. I hope she never has to meet the Queen, because her curtsy would probably end up as a kind of headbutt and Chloe might get arrested.

'No, no,' I agreed. 'No ball games, no team games.'

'I hate team games,' sighed Chloe. 'People always think I'm the nerd.'

'You are so not the nerd!' I whispered indignantly. 'I'm the nerd! Whenever I try sports, my thighs kind of stick together. I hate team games anyway, except when played by gorgeous men with rippling torsos.'

'Oh yeah!' smiled Chloe. 'Remember that beach rugby in Newquay?'

Remember it? Little did Chloe know that approximately every five minutes ever since, I'd thought wistfully of Beast racing across the sands. God, he was such a legend! I remembered how his black curls had danced in the sea breeze, and his grey-green eyes always seemed so restless and interested in everything. School had become a deserted dungeon since he'd left. There was no longer any chance that I'd bump into him in the corridor, and now I was tragically haunted by all the places where I'd bumped into him last year, when I hadn't even realised how fabulous he was, so it had been a total waste of bumpingness.

'What are you thinking about?' asked Chloe sharply. I had clearly started to wear a foolish faraway grin. I hadn't told her I was mad about Beast, because it was a slightly dodgy subject: Chloe had been mad about Beast herself, all last term, before the summer hols. I'd have to get round to telling her soon, when I thought she could cope with it.

'Nothing, nothing.' I shook myself out of my reverie. 'I'm just thinking how wonderful it'll be to get fit. So when do we start the exercise? And it can't be jogging. You can get something called "Jogger's Nipple" and I'd die rather than have to go and see the doctor about that!'

'Aerobics!' yelled Chloe. People at nearby tables looked startled.

'Sssssh!' I warned. Thank goodness Maria was in the kitchen.

'We can get a DVD and do it secretly at home!' whispered Chloe. 'If we did it every day, would we start to see results in seven days?'

'Of course!' I was wondering how Beast would react to a new, slim, fit me. 'We'd start seeing results from Day One! And we can take photos of ourselves before we start, and once we've transformed ourselves we can take After Photos. And we must be totally honest with each other about what we look like.'

'Yeah,' agreed Chloe. 'In fact, we must be honest with each other about everything.' I gulped guiltily here, because of Chloe being in the dark about my feelings for Beast.

'We need a deadline,' I suggested, because I wanted to steer the conversation away from honesty. 'You know, a big event we can prepare for, so we'll have to be amazing by then. Hey! How about Jailhouse Rock?'

Jailhouse Rock was this amazing rock concert Beast was helping to organise, scheduled to take place in about four weeks' time in the Sir George Plunkett Memorial Concert Bowl, known to one and all as Plunkett. It was being organised *by* Young People *for* Young People, in aid of Amnesty International (hence the name Jailhouse Rock – because Amnesty supports prisoners all over the world who are unjustly in jail only for speaking out against bad governments).

'Jailhouse Rock!' exclaimed Chloe. 'Perfect! We have to be there anyway. We'll arrive looking like a million dollars.'

'We'll blow everybody away.' I nodded. I was secretly wondering how much of a transformation I'd need to undergo to blow Beast away. The trouble was, once upon a time, he had actually asked me out – back in the grim old dark ages when I'd hated him, and I'd told him I wouldn't go out with him if he was the last man left alive.

And though he'd been polite since then, whenever we'd met, I realised that he was never going to refer to it ever again: the whole episode had been hastily wiped from his memory banks. I felt sure he wouldn't ask me out again if *I* was the last *girl* left alive. We were going to remain on chilly but polite terms until the end of time – unless I managed to transform myself into such a goddess that he would completely lose control, forget about the past, and throw himself at me at a hundred and seventy miles per hour.

Chloe doodled on the margins of her notebook. She drew a massive pair of goddess-like eyes. Maria arrived at our table and pointedly took away our empty mugs. We were going to have to queue for some new snacks or vacate our snug little corner.

'Anything else you think we should put on this list? As in, kind of basic principles?' I asked. 'I mean, I've not really done enough research into goddesses . . .'

'Oh, only that boys are going to be totally off the map!' said Chloe firmly. 'No crushes, no falling head over heels, not even a piddling little minor half-hearted moment of fancying a guy until we've transformed into goddesses, OK? We've wasted so much time thinking about boys in the past! From now on, we won't even notice if Ben Jones sits next to us in the canteen!'

'Ben Jones?' I asked playfully. 'Who's he?' Ben Jones is the school dreamboat, the male equivalent of eye candy, and normally I'd be quite happy to join in a bit of drooling over him, even though, of course, since I'd secretly become obsessed with Beast, nobody else was even slightly interesting.

'So boys are *out*!' insisted Chloe.

'Absolutely!' I agreed, secretly indulging myself in a little tiny thought about Beast's lovely strong masculine hands. 'But, Chloe – what if . . . ?'

In a sudden feverish fantasy, Beast turned up on my doorstep, just like he had last summer, and asked me out. And this time I didn't tell him to get lost . . .

'No what ifs!' insisted Chloe. She can be so headstrong at times. 'Boys are off the menu while we concentrate on ourselves. It's pathetic to measure ourselves by our success with boys anyway. We should be powerful, independent females in our own right – right?'

I nodded, trying to look powerful and independent

but secretly promising myself a tiny little indulgent thought about Beast as soon as Chloe got distracted by something. Maybe in a minute she would decide she wanted a Dolphin Cafe brownie or cinnamon toast.

A shadow fell across our table. We looked up. A pale, pasty boy stood there with beige slicked-back hair and khaki eyes. Oh God! It was Matthew Kesterton. If we wanted to be completely indifferent to boys, Matthew was the perfect candidate to begin our project. We'd got to know him a few months ago in circumstances too embarrassing to explain here. Oh, all right then: we'd pretended to be life coaches and Matthew had been our only client. He was basically the kind of guy who gets the Nobel Prize for Nerdhood. I had wasted a whole afternoon of my life trying to teach him how to smile.

'Hi, gels,' he said in a faux South London accent. 'May I join you?' And his lips twitched upwards in a kind of snarl of agony. I could see he still hadn't got the hang of smiling.

Chapter 2

'Hey! Matthew! Great to see you! How was your summer?' I indicated graciously that the third chair was at his disposal. Matthew sat down carefully, as if he had never actually done it before, but had read a pamphlet entitled *How to Lower Yourself into a Chair*. I smiled treacherously – it was so *not* great to see him. I would rather have been joined by a ten-foot boa constrictor – a creature considerably less cold-blooded than Matthew.

'It's Paolo, actually,' he announced pompously. 'I've changed my name. I think Matthew sounds a bit old-fashioned.'

This was a major style error on Matthew's part, though I was too polite to say so. I have a snobbish taste for old-fashioned names. Harry, for example. It is, incidentally, Beast's real name: Harry Hawkins. Beat that for charisma! It sounds a bit like a pirate, but then, he looks a bit like a pirate, sometimes.

'Right,' I said mischievously. 'OK, er, Paolo. I've changed my name, too. I'm . . . Doris.' I couldn't help myself: Matthew brings out the sarcastic worst in me. Chloe looked startled. 'And Chloe's changed her name to Vera. How was your summer, then, Ma— Paolo?'

'Oh, it was great, yeah,' droned Matthew in his strange dull voice. 'First I did a life-saving course . . .' I didn't like that word *first*. It suggested we might have to sit through a whole catalogue of very worthy things Matthew had done throughout the summer hols.

'Oh brilliant, well done,' I said. 'So you can save lives, now, can you?'

'Uh-huh,' said Matthew, evidently deep in some kind of fantasy of being a lifeguard in Atlantic City.

'How wonderful!' gasped Chloe, avoiding my eye. 'So if we were drowning, you could save us!' I knew exactly what she was thinking: that she'd rather drown, any day, than see Matthew laboriously approaching through the waves like some earnest podgy seal hell-bent on watery courtship.

'I'm not sure if I could save you both.' Matthew looked puzzled. 'Especially if you clung to me in panic.'

'I promise,' I said seriously, 'that I will never cling to you in panic.' Matthew looked slightly disappointed.

'Nor will I,' promised Chloe fervently. It was the first honest thing we'd said since he sat down.

Chloe and I avoided looking at each other. We were going to have such a laugh about this later.

'I think it's wonderful, being a lifeguard,' I said. 'I really admire you for it, Ma— Paolo.'

'We ought to learn how to do it, too, really,' said Chloe.

'I can do mouth-to-mouth as well,' said Matthew, 'so if either of you girls ever goes into a coma, let me know.' He gave a weird Martian-style smile at this point, so I think this was supposed to be a rather sleazy and unpleasant joke.

'Yeah, we should do a life-saving course, Chloe,' I suggested.

'There's one every Thursday at the leisure centre,' said Matthew. 'Run by St John Ambulance.'

'Oh dear!' I dived in quick. 'We can't make Thursdays, because that's the night we go out with

19

our boyfriends.' I thought I'd better get a couple of imaginary boyfriends lined up quick, after all that unnecessary ghastliness about mouth-to-mouth resuscitation.

'Boyfriends?' enquired Matthew, trying not to look crushed. We were probably the only girls he'd ever spoken to in his life. I knew he preferred me to Chloe, because once he'd said so, which was a terrible kind of curse rather than a compliment. 'Anybody I know?'

'I'm not sure,' I said. 'Do you know Daniel Stringer?' I thought Daniel sounded nice and manly and James Bond-ish.

'Daniel? Uh, yeah, I think I did meet him once,' said Matthew. This was a major surprise, because I had only just invented Daniel. 'How is he these days?'

I felt panicky and furious that Matthew had managed to wrong-foot me by trumping my outrageous lie with an even more outrageous one of his own.

'Oh, Daniel's fine,' I said irritably. I hated Daniel slightly for having met Matthew behind my back, before I'd ever invented him. In fact I was already planning to dump him. 'You know what he's like . . .'

I challenged Matthew with a direct glare, but he just smiled and nodded. Maybe he actually *did* know somebody called Daniel Stringer! 'Chloe's boyfriend is the class act, though,' I went on, inspired suddenly. 'He's American.'

Matthew looked impressed. 'What's his name?' he asked, turning to her. Chloe's gaze became fixed. You could see she couldn't think of a single boy's name, poor lamb – she was frozen in the headlamps of my ludicrous fantasy.

'Tom . . . Cruise,' she spluttered. I covered her embarrassment with a huge laugh.

'That's what we call him, secretly, behind his back,' I explained. 'His real name's Tom Cribbins.' I realised this didn't sound very American. 'Cribbins-Goldfarb,' I added hastily. 'His father is the president of some bank in New York.'

'Nice job,' said Matthew. 'I'd like to meet him. I'm thinking of going into banking. That's where the big bucks are.'

'Matthew!' I said with flirty reproachfulness. 'I mean, Paolo! You mustn't become too much of a material boy, you know. Girls like a man with a heart.'

'Oh, I do a lot of charity work,' he boasted. 'And I

know girls like that sort of thing, because that's how I met my current girlfriend.' Chloe and I were instantly fascinated. Had Matthew really got a *real* girlfriend? Or was he just joining us in the Fibbing for England Olympic Team?

'Tell us about her!' Chloe begged.

'Her name is Trixiebell Dixon-Bright,' he said. 'She's a tap dancer and oboist.' We were stunned. Game, set and match to Matthew. 'I was just wondering,' Matthew went on, 'if you might be available to help out in a different charity project I'm involved in – it would only be a couple of nights a week, and it doesn't have to be Thursdays.'

'Oh, I'm sorry,' I said hastily. 'We're busy with . . .' I momentarily forgot the names of our boyfriends '. . . stuff with . . . Dan and . . .'

'Tom,' Chloe prompted me, a tiny hint of alarm in her eyes.

'. . . every night of the week at the moment.' I grasped wildly for some ultra-important project. 'Thursday is our night off with the guys,' I went on recklessly, 'but for the rest of the week we're incredibly busy making sleeping bags for the homeless.'

'Out of recycled materials,' added Chloe quickly, 'which Tom collects in his pick-up truck.'

Just at this moment, some boys sitting over by the window lifted up their heads and howled like dogs. My heart nearly jumped right out of my mouth. This could only mean one thing – *Beast was walking past*!

I gasped, I choked, and with a flash of genius, though I say it myself, I turned that little choke into a fully-fledged coughing fit, muttered 'excuse me' and stumbled for the door. I had to get a glimpse of Beast! Just a five-second peep at his divine back disappearing down the street would be enough! I burst out through the door of the Dolphin Cafe, and oh, horror! I almost cannoned right into the arms of Beast himself, who was coming up the steps, accompanied, disastrously, by a girl with long eyelashes, tawny skin, glorious brown curly hair and a figure to die for. In other words, somebody who was a goddess *already*.

Chapter 3

I racked my brains for an alluring remark, but the cupboard was bare. All I could muster was the charismatic aside *'I'm having a coughing fit'* but even that came out back to front.

'I'm having a foff—' I gasped. Oh no! The coughing fit had become a foffing kit! I burst past Beast and the girl, coughing and foffing a whole lot more, and ran a few yards down the street without turning round. I didn't want Beast to be too concerned about the cough, though – after all, he was going to be a doctor one day – so I slapped my chest a few times and stared at a nearby shop window as if to indicate that my foff was not life-threatening enough to affect my interest in merchandise.

I noticed a burning pain in my throat which

suggested that, though I might not have had a real cough to start off with, I had almost certainly ruptured my larynx in my foolish attempt to catch a glimpse of my Unattainable Beloved. I don't think real goddesses ever have that kind of trouble.

I turned back to the Dolphin Cafe and rejoined Chloe and Matthew, scanning the room casually for Beast and the girl. They were standing at the counter, and I was alarmed to see that their elbows were actually touching as they admired Maria's display of pastries. My own elbows tingled jealously at the sight.

Matthew was in the middle of a seemingly endless saga about Trixiebell's next oboe recital, so I just sat down and tried not to look insane with anxiety when Beast loomed over our table. He and the girl were carrying takeaway drinks.

'Uh, hi there, Beast,' said Matthew. Oh no! Matthew knew him! 'This is – uhh, Doris and Vera. This is Beast Hawkins.' Nightmare! Bad enough that this laborious idiot was presuming to introduce us to Beast, but the ridiculous names! Beast looked surprised, but with an adorable little rippling smile that he was trying to suppress.

'Well, guys, this is Charlie,' he said. 'Charlie, this

is Paolo, Vera and er, apparently – Doris.' Beast glanced at me, and winked. Oh my God! My poor little heart turned a somersault! What did he mean by it? It seemed like a secret sign, as if we two shared an understanding.

The girl Charlie smiled. Her teeth were perfect. An elegant hint of gold twinkled in her ears – tiny earrings shaped like crescent moons.

'Hi,' she said. 'Hi, Doris, hi, Vera!' I decided I had to end this madness. We must ditch the names.

'We're really called Zoe and Chloe,' I said, but my voice came out as a horrid croak. I seemed to have genuinely damaged my vocal cords during my coughing fit. 'Sorry – my voice is a bit weird. The names were just a joke.' A flicker of amusement twinkled in Beast's lovely grey-green eyes.

'We're thinking of trying out some new names,' explained Chloe.

'Doris and Vera were just a kitsch retro moment,' I added.

'What a great idea!' grinned Charlie. She turned to Beast. 'We should change our names, too!' Oh no! They were a *we*! A cold, curdled feeling spread through my intestines. I felt sick. I would never eat again. Although I might just possibly have to eat

Charlie – if there was no other way of getting rid of her. 'Hey, Beast!' she went on. 'I think you're more of a James.'

How dare Charlie take liberties with Beast and tell him he was a James? She was so wrong about that, as well. He was way too rugged for a James. Jameses tend to be kind of smooth and polished, in my experience. Anyway, I knew he was a secret Harry. I wondered if she knew, too. The way she looked at him, it seemed as if she might know all his secrets.

'I asked Zoe and Chloe to help with the Amnesty gig,' Matthew droned on. Oh no, no, *no*! In our attempt to keep Matthew at bay, we'd just unwittingly refused to help with Beast's Jailhouse Rock concert! 'But they can't, because they're busy every night with their boyfriends,' concluded Matthew, winning the Award for the Most Tactless Blunders Crammed into One Short Speech.

'Their . . . boyfriends?' asked Beast, raising his eyebrows with a teasing smile, directed mostly at Chloe.

'Dan and Tom,' Matthew informed him matter-of-factly. Matthew had now destroyed my life, and I began to wonder if he was Satan in human form. Well, almost human, anyway – it would explain the strange khaki eyes.

'Boyfriends, eh?' Beast went on, 'Anybody I know? Where did you meet them? Newquay?'

'No,' said Chloe, floundering a bit. She used to have a thing about Beast and she's still slightly awkward with him sometimes. Also, she's not at her best when free-range lying. 'We met them through the homeless thingummyjig.'

'What? Are they homeless?' asked Beast, looking deeply puzzled and quizzical.

'No,' said Matthew, who appeared to have become our PR spokesman in the most annoying way. 'In fact, Chloe's boyfriend Tom is from the Goldfarb banking family in New York, you know. Hey – maybe Tom's bank can sponsor the rock concert?' Matthew looked appealingly at Chloe. Chloe cringed and shook her head.

'It's not the sponsorship I'm worried about,' said Beast with a sigh. He glanced out anxiously through the cafe window at the passing traffic. 'If things get any worse I'll be changing my name to José Olivera and disappearing to South America.'

'What do you mean?' I asked, in a concerned croak. 'Are you having problems with Jailhouse Rock?' Poor Beast! He worked so hard. I couldn't bear to think of things going wrong for him.

'Where do I start?' he shrugged, with a self-deprecating smile. 'My entrepreneurial skills have deserted me. I'm convinced my boss is going to sack me any moment.'

'Who is your boss?' asked Chloe.

'Arnold Brown,' said Beast. 'Managing Director of Major Events.'

'Well, don't worry,' I quipped, trying to cheer Beast up. 'If Arnie sacks you, we'll kill him!' Beast gave me an amused look.

'You'll get some hassle from Charlie, then,' he warned. 'He's her uncle!'

This was serious news. I'd made an embarrassing blunder, boasting about my homicidal skills being applied to Charlie's uncle. And if she was the boss's niece, it would pile all sorts of pressure on to poor Beast. If she hit on him, how could he refuse?

'Sorry, Charlie!' I assured her. 'But if we do have to kill your unc we'll do it very gently and vegetarianly with velvet gloves on.'

'Oh, don't bother!' replied Charlie. 'He deserves it sometimes – he's a monster. But then my family are all mad. I'm totally crazy!' She threw her head back, closed her eyes and pressed her fingers against her brow in what was clearly designed to be a crazy-but-irresistible pose. Matthew laughed. I guessed he would be practising that pose in front of his mirror all evening. I hoped so, anyway. I couldn't wait to see his version of it.

'And then there's Rose Quartz,' said Beast.

'God!' I blurted out. 'I was so amazed when I heard you'd got Rose Quartz! I told Tam last night and she almost choked on her lasagne!'

'Is Tam home, then?' asked Beast. 'I haven't seen her for ages. How is she?'

Beast is a good mate of my older sister. In fact he kind of saved her life last summer because he realised she'd got appendicitis and called an ambulance and stuff.

'Oh, Tam's great,' I assured him. 'She's just home for a couple of days . . . But Rose Quartz – getting her to top the bill in Jailhouse Rock is such a major coup! She's got to be in the top ten artistes world-wide! There's no room on her mantelpiece for any more Grammys!'

'Yes, but . . .' Beast's face clouded over. 'She's started messing me about. First she said yes, then she suddenly remembered a gig in Sydney which might clash, then she said it would be OK after all because she'd managed to juggle the flights, but now she's going cold on the idea because she thinks she'll have jet lag. I keep telling her she can't pull out because her name's on the posters – she doesn't know there aren't even any posters yet, because the guy who was supposed to design them has lost the plot.'

'Oh my God!' I croaked. 'How horrible for you!' Poor Beast looked so stressed – even though his frown did increase his rugged good looks, I preferred to see him smiley and happy. I longed to leap right out of my chair and cradle him in my arms – for about ten years.

'Don't worry about Rose Quartz,' said Charlie firmly. 'She's just playing hard to get. She fancied you, I could tell.' Oh God! Charlie had been with Beast when they had *actually met* Rose Quartz! Maybe Charlie never left his side! She was certainly looking a bit jealous. 'Rose was hoping you'd apply for the job of toy boy,' said Charlie with a sly grin that was kind of edgy and tormented. But her torment couldn't compare to mine. Charlie only had to worry about Rose Quartz. I had to worry about Rose *and* Charlie.

'Maybe we could help . . . ?' I ventured.

'You could join my leafleting team!' said Matthew with a horrid triumphant pounce. 'Distribute the flyers! Get shops to display the posters!'

'Zoe!' snapped Chloe. 'We can't! We're totally committed to Dan and Tom! Those homeless people need their sleeping bags! Winter is coming!'

I glanced irritably at Chloe. I might have to kill her just slightly for mentioning those fictitious boyfriends again. I might have to murder her toenails or her hair or something.

'There aren't any posters yet, anyway,' sighed Beast.

'Wait! I've got it!' gasped Charlie. 'We could have a competition among local schools! The winning design could be used for the poster!'

'Brilliant!' said Matthew. Beast looked more uncertain.

'Could we get it done in time, though?' he pondered. 'Those posters have to be out within a month. The schools . . .'

'I'll ring them all!' promised Charlie. 'I'll email them all! My mum's a teacher – I'll force her to get her class to do something. I'll work night and day! I'll never stop! It'll be brilliant, I promise! When I get excited about something, no power on Earth can stop me!' She gazed at Beast with adoration. He gave her one of those brave but slightly disbelieving smiles and put his arm round her shoulders for a moment.

'Thanks, babe,' he smiled wearily. 'You're a star!'

I almost passed out from sheer anguish.

Chapter 4

Ten minutes later, Beast and Charlie had gone off to organise the poster competition and Chloe and I were walking home. Matthew, luckily, was travelling in the other direction, and I was hoping to keep things like that for the rest of our lives.

'Poor Beast!' I said. 'I thought that everything he touched turned to gold, but this Jailhouse Rock thing seems to be driving him over the edge. Why don't we give him a hand?'

'No!' Chloe snapped. 'Listen, Zoe, I have bad vibes about Amnesty and Beast.'

'What?!' I panicked. I needed Chloe to be completely cool about Beast, or I'd never be able to confide in her.

'You remember last term, when I was mad about

him,' said Chloe between gritted teeth. 'He asked me to take part in that vigil in aid of Amnesty, yeah? In the high street? In a sort of cage, like a prison cell type thing, all night? And I thought it was going to be just him and me but there were two other people there and he was, like, flirting with this other girl all night? And anyway . . . whenever I see Beast I think of all those nuisance love texts I sent him and I just cringe for England. That was soooo embarrassing! His mum even saw one!'

'Yeah, but, Chloe, all this is ancient history. You've got to move on.'

'I have moved on! I don't care about boys any more! I'm a free spirit! And we're reinventing our-selves! Girls to goddesses, remember?'

'It hasn't exactly been a brilliant start,' I grumbled. 'That was so cringe-making! Getting totally tied up in a stupid web of ridiculous lies.'

'You started it! Telling Matthew that we'd changed our names and got boyfriends!' I had to admit this was true. I was so regretting it now. Beast thought I had a boyfriend called Dan and I was busy with him every night of the week. 'Anyway,' Chloe went on, 'I don't mind Beast thinking I've got a boyfriend.' It was ironical how different our feelings were.

'We could help for just, say, one night a week. It wouldn't hurt . . .' I gabbled in desperation.

'No, Zoe! We have to keep clear of all that! Imagine having to work with Matthew anyway! What a nightmare! I never want to spend five minutes with him again as long as I live!'

I didn't argue any more. I started to wonder if I could somehow help Beast once a week without Chloe knowing. Maybe I could invent violin lessons or something. It would seem fairly insignificant to lie to her about something so minor, compared to the massive betrayal of keeping her in the dark about my feelings for Beast. I began to feel I would never be able to tell her about that, and even if I ended up married to Beast, he'd have to go upstairs and hide in the wardrobe every time she came round.

I became preoccupied with a delicious fantasy about being married to Beast and living beside a lake, where we swam every morning before barbecuing our breakfast on the shore. I wasn't really listening to what Chloe was saying, and when I tuned back into her, I discovered I had agreed to a total overhaul of her wardrobe.

'You've always thought my clothes were hopeless,'

said Chloe. 'Now's your chance. Be totally honest. I'll accept every word you say. You'll be my style advisor. We'll chuck out all the rubbish and make me magnificent. Turning ourselves into goddesses in seven days is gonna be a piece of cake – at least style-wise!'

'OK,' I agreed hesitantly. I was beginning to get hungry and had been looking forward to walking on home after we reached Chloe's house, and making myself a massive cheese and tomato sandwich.

But it was true: I *had* always thought Chloe's fashion sense needed sharpening up a bit. Maybe this was an opportunity too good to waste. It might take us more than seven days to improve our actual bods, but the right clothes can instantly transform even hopeless nerds – think Gok Wan.

'OK,' said Chloe, as we entered her bedroom. 'So, tell me: where do I start?' She flung open her wardrobe doors and I sat down on her bed. A riot of ghastly colour flooded out of her wardrobe and enveloped me in visual noise.

'Right . . .' I got up and pulled out a yellow dress with a pattern of orange tortoises on it. 'When did you last wear this?'

'Ah.' Chloe's eyes had a faraway look. 'At my Auntie Angela's in Dorset, years ago. What's wrong with it?'

I sighed. 'Where do I start? It's yellow, which is about your worst colour, it has tortoises on it, which let's face it are best left in the wild, and it has a weird full skirt which probably makes you look like a lampshade.' Chloe looked cross.

'Auntie Angela loved it!' she said rebelliously.

'But, Chloe, that was years ago. You were just a kid. You need a more sophisticated look now. Chuck it out.'

'I can't chuck it out! Don't be so harsh! This dress reminds me of that holiday. I had the best time in this dress. I almost kissed my cousin Jack.'

'OK, OK, leave that one.' Hastily I hung it back in the wardrobe. If Chloe wanted her clothes collection to be like Tutankhamen's tomb, that was up to her. Instead I took out a pair of lime-green dungarees.

'Yeah, that's more like it,' said Chloe, nodding eagerly as if she thought I was about to give her an award or something. 'You've always said green is my best colour.'

'But not this green! This is vile!'

Chloe burst into tears. 'My dad brought those back for me from Dubai!' she cried. 'They're not vile!'

'Sorry, sorry, I didn't mean vile,' I back-pedalled at speed. 'I was going to say . . . viol-*ent*. The green . . . it's a bit harsh. Probably in Dubai they have lovely bright sunlight, and so . . . this colour would look less . . . would look better. In this country, though . . .' I continued cautiously '. . . I would go for maybe sage green, or sea green. Either of those would make you look fabulous.'

The dungarees went back in the wardrobe. I didn't dare say anything about dungarees as a form of clothing. Chloe had stopped crying and was just sniffing now, even though it was a very indignant sniff. I hesitated between a red, green and yellow T-shirt and a skirt with horrible frills in bright, shiny crimson. I chose the latter. I could feel Chloe tense up as I held it to the light.

'This is a cute skirt,' I lied, 'but basically *shiny* is a bit tacky, Clo. Except for evenings.'

'I only wear it in the evenings.'

'How many times have you worn it?'

'Loads of times.' She was lying. I remembered when she had bought it, back last spring, and how I'd had to bite my lip.

'I've never seen you in it.'

'I wear it when you're not there! Because I know you'd be secretly sneering about it!'

'I'm not sneering! Chloe, you asked me to do this!'

'I didn't realise you'd be so horrible about it!'

'I'm not being horrible! Anyway, once we've done your wardrobe and cleared it out, you can come over to my house and go through mine!' Chloe looked slightly comforted for a moment. I turned back to the crimson, shiny, flouncy skirt.

'Basically,' I said, trying to sound loving and gentle, 'this skirt would be fine as a party piece, but on somebody else.'

'Who?' demanded Chloe furiously. 'You, I suppose?'

'No, no!' I laughed (I wouldn't be seen dead in it). 'Not me. I'm too fat. Somebody tall and slim and dark, uhhh . . . Alice Clarke, maybe.'

'Why shouldn't I wear it?' snapped Chloe.

'First, crimson isn't the best colour for redheads. It clashes with your hair. You should go for greens and blues and autumnal colours.'

'Boring!' shouted Chloe.

'Secondly,' I went on, determined now because she was starting to irritate me, 'a flouncy skirt is fine on a tall girl, but on somebody short, you get the toad-stool effect.'

'Don't you call me a freakin' toadstool!' shouted Chloe.

'Stop shouting!' I hissed. 'I'm not saying you look like a toadstool! I'm just saying flouncy skirts can look like that on short girls!'

'I'm not short!' snarled Chloe. I didn't reply to this, I just looked down on her puny five-foot-two frame from my towering height of five foot six or sevenish.

'Chloe, I'm just trying to help you,' I pleaded. 'On the way here you asked me to go through your wardrobe. You said I'd be your style advisor and it would be my job to make you magnificent and you'd accept every word I said.' Chloe just glared. I advanced on the wardrobe again and hung the skirt back up. I was determined to have my say.

'Look . . .' I ran my hand along her clothes. 'Bright blue, bright red, yellow, pink, patterns, logos, prints, checks . . . this T-shirt even has a goddam hamster on it.'

'That hamster's not goddam!' shrieked Chloe. 'He's called Hammy! He was my best friend for two years at primary school! I used to talk to him secretly so I didn't feel lonely! Nobody would speak to me sometimes just because I had red hair!'

'OK, OK, forget Hammy,' I soothed. 'All I wanted to say is, just take a look at all these bright colours and patterns and stuff – it looks like a children's party. If you want to be magnificent and a goddess and all that, you're going to have to stop decorating yourself like a Christmas tree and get some plain, stylish stuff for a change.'

'Well, you can go to hell!' Chloe's eyes flashed and sparked. 'You think you know it all! You think you're so clever and freakin' elegant and stuff! Well, you're not! You're fat and spotty and your ears are weird!'

This was too much. Something snapped. I turned on my heel, marched out of her bedroom and down the stairs. If I'd been in my own home I'd have slammed the door, but Chloe's mum Fran was in the kitchen and being in somebody else's house does rather cramp your style when it comes to volcanic rage.

I walked home fuming and nervous. I knew I was fat and spotty, but what was this about my ears? Chloe was such a bitch. All I'd done was try to give her some style advice – when asked, mind you – and she'd given me a whole new thing to be self-conscious about. I couldn't wait to get home and take a long hard look at my ears.

Chapter 5

Mum was out, so I'd be spared a homework lecture. Great! Dad was busy in the kitchen. I gave him a brief hug and enquired if he'd had a good day.

'No, it's been a disaster, old boy,' he said. He always calls me that, because they thought I was going to be a boy. 'But, hey!' Dad went on. 'I'm making us a high-calorie supper. Mum's in Glasgow inspecting a burned-out warehouse, so while the cat's away . . .' He tapped the side of his nose and winked. 'I'm making beef and mushroom pie, with mash!'

'Wow! Brilliant!' I cheered up slightly, but I was still feeling stressed out because of my row with Chloe. I needed to patch things up with her, and fast. Maybe I'd been a bit too harsh about her weird clothes sense. In fact, it's one of the things I love about her, so why had I droned on patronisingly about plain elegance? All the same . . . 'Dad,' I asked, 'can you see anything weird about my ears?'

'Nope,' said Dad decisively. 'They're beautiful. They're perfect. They are, of course, the Morris ears, inherited from me: small, streamlined for wind-resistance, and worn fashionably close to the head.' He kissed me on the head and turned back to his pie.

I was not completely reassured, though. I raced upstairs. Music was coming from Tam's room. I found her sitting on the floor surrounded by clothes. She spends seventy per cent of her time like this.

'Hi, Zoe,' she smiled. 'How was school? And have you seen my dark-blue camisole top with sparkly bits?'

'Ooops. Borrowed it at the weekend, I'll get it right now,' I promised, diving to my room and grabbing it out of a pile of dirty laundry.

'Thanks . . .' said Tam absent-mindedly. 'I'm trying to sort stuff out, and sell a load of old things . . . So how was your day?'

I told her about the row with Chloe and my futile attempt to change her fashion sense. 'We're trying to transform ourselves into goddesses in seven days,' I sighed. 'We're never going to manage it. How can

Chloe be a goddess dressed in five different random colours that clash?'

'Oh, that's just Chloe,' laughed Tam.

'And, Tam, she said my ears were weird! Look at them . . . tell me what's wrong with them!'

Tam stared at my ears from every direction, frowning slightly.

'Don't frown!' I begged.

'Sorry, sorry,' said Tam. 'Your ears are fine. They're a bit small, maybe, and close to your head, but I'd kill for ears like that. Mine are like elephant ears – look!' She pulled back thick hanks of blonde hair to reveal her rather large velvety ears, adorned with glittering earrings of the silver dangly sort. 'I'm saving up to have surgery!' she whispered. 'I want to have my ears pinned back nearer to my head. Every time I wear my hair up I look like a goddam silver cup at a sports day!'

'Well, when you have your ear op,' I said, 'maybe they could transplant one of your ears on to my head. I mean, do a swap. So we'd both have one tiny weird ear and one elephant one!' Tam agreed, grabbed a pencil and drew a cartoon of us with our odd ears. We looked hilarious. I grabbed the pencil and added a massive zit on my chin. Tam grabbed it back and gave herself an enormous nose like an anteater. I was giggling uncontrollably now. I wrestled the pencil back and gave myself massive saggy boobs.

'Mum and Dad . . . ?' gasped Tam, shaking with laughter, and drew Dad as a cute little pig and Mum as a fearsome power-dressed rat.

Still laughing, I crawled up on to Tam's bed and she sprawled out on the floor. For a moment I felt what bliss it was to be laughing with Tam, and how I was going to miss her when she went back to uni.

'So, Zoe,' Tam said after a while, 'apart from this thing with Chloe, how's life? Who's your latest squeeze?'

'Nobody,' I said, a bit too fast. 'Chloe and I are going through a self-improvement programme. We're going to give ourselves the mother of all makeovers. We don't have time for boys right now.'

'Oh yeah?' grinned Tam. 'How long will that last? Half an hour?'

I couldn't tell her about my feelings for Beast. He was a bit too close to Tam for me ever to admit anything to her. She might try a bit of matchmaking or something. It could end in disaster.

'There is *one* thing I was wondering, though,' I said. I was still in anguish about those fictional boyfriends I'd invented and what Beast might be thinking about it, if anything.

'If you were crazy about somebody . . .' I began. Tam sat up quickly, looking eager and grinning.

'Ye-e-eah . . . ?'

'And he hadn't, well, hadn't, uh, made a move, exactly, but you were hoping . . . I mean, do you think it would be a good idea if he thought some other guy was interested in you?'

'Who is it, Zoe?' Tam beamed, ignoring my question and joining me on the bed. 'Who's the lucky boy?'

'Nobody!' I retorted in panic, sitting up and trying to compose my face into serene calmness, even though my heart was beating quite fast.

'Come on! There is somebody!' Tam peeped round into my face. Her eyes were dancing. I was so wishing I'd never started this.

'No, there isn't,' I said, blushing. 'It's just – in theory. What do you think?'

Tam's face was full of mischief, but she hesitated for a moment or two, thinking, and in that little pause we heard footsteps coming upstairs. Dad was obviously going to announce that dinner was almost ready and frankly, it wouldn't be a moment too soon.

There was a knock on the door. But it wasn't Dad's knock. This was a more polite knock, more hesitant.

'Tam?' A male voice called softly. It could have been any of Tam's mates: Ginger, Smiffy, Morton, Christo, Ape . . .

'Come in!' shouted Tam. The door opened – and Beast came in! Every bone in my body turned into noodle soup. It was a major task to stop myself from melting away down the cracks in Tam's floorboards in little rivulets of red-hot panic.

Beast gave me a sudden wonderful smile, like the sun coming out. My poor little heart skipped in the warmth, like a spring lamb.

'Hi again, Zoe,' he said, then hesitated for a moment and turned to Tam. 'Hey, Tam! Your dad said to come on up. I heard you were home from uni and I just wanted to drop in and say hello. How are you?'

Tam jumped up and hugged him. I sat there on the bed feeling a bit awkward. It was so unfair that Tam, who was just a friend of his, could enjoy a massive cuddle, whilst I, who adored him more than words can express, had to just sit there and watch.

Though tormented by the sight of Beast's arms around my glamorous sister, it did at least give me time to try to return my bones to their solid state and cover my weird ears with a few little strands of wiry hair.

'I saw Zoe earlier in the Dolphin Cafe,' said Beast, glancing at me with a fleeting smile, at which ten thousand of my goose pimples throbbed with excitement. 'She told me you were home, and I realised it's been ages since I last saw you. Are you OK?'

'Yeah, thanks, brilliant,' replied Tam tossing her wonderful blonde hair to demonstrate her post-appendicitis health. 'But how are you? And how's Jailhouse Rock coming on? I'll be there, of course – I'm going to organise a whole busload of my mates from uni!'

'Awesome,' said Beast. 'You're an angel.' He beamed at her, and I stared up in fascination at his profile, trying to commit it to my memory in a kind of secret mental photo. I find that, though I've known Beast for years, since I started to be mad about him, when he's not there I can't remember what he looks like.

'Sit down, sit down!' cried Tam, sweeping some bras off her computer chair. Beast sat down, but as if he wasn't planning to stay long. I hoped he would find time to bestow another of his casual smiles on me, because it was at least a minute since the last one and I was desperate for a refill. 'You've just arrived at the perfect moment!' Tam prattled on. 'I was interrogating Zoe about her latest boyfriend! She won't tell me who he is! Come on, Zoe – tell Beast. Maybe he can give you some tips! Hey, Beast, Zoe wants to know, if this guy she's mad about finds out she's going out with another guy, will it make him more interested, or less?'

Chapter 6

Tam beamed teasingly at me. She had ceased to be my adorable sister and had become some kind of torturing fiend from the deepest pits of hell. Beast shot me a quizzical look.

'I've heard about this guy already,' said Beast. 'Dan, wasn't it?' My heart broke with a resounding crack which registered in the earthquake tracking station in faraway Antarctica. I had to end this Dan madness right now: I had to explain to Beast that I didn't have a boyfriend called Dan – that I didn't have a boyfriend at all, but I had to do it without sounding lonely or nerdy. Above all, it mustn't sound like an obvious come-on.

'Uhh . . .' I faltered. It was a challenge to find the right words, and for a split second I just hesitated while my mind raced.

'Dan!?' Tam pounced. 'Dan who? What? Where? Which Dan? Not Dan Gibbons?'

'No!' I screamed. Dan Gibbons is a ghastly monster from school who is obsessed with motor-bikes.

I instantly realised that by screaming '*no*' I had made it sound as if my Dan was a real, superior alter-native to Dan Gibbons.

'Come on, Zoe!' coaxed Tam. 'Tell us about him! Is he at Ashcroft? Or one of the posh schools? Or is he at uni somewhere? Where did you meet him?'

'Yeah, come on,' said Beast. 'Put us out of our misery! Who's the guy?'

'Nobody!' I spluttered. 'The thing is – the thing was, we'd . . .' I was about to tell them how Chloe and I had had to invent fictional boyfriends, but at this very moment, disastrously, my moby rang. I grabbed it and headed for the door.

'Hey!' giggled Tam. 'Maybe this is lover-boy right now! Grab the phone, Beast, and ask him if his intentions are honourable!'

'It's Chloe!' I yelled, and rushed to my room. I needed to talk to Chloe but not now, for goodness' sake, not right now! Not during these sacred few minutes while Beast was actually in our house!

'Zoe?' Chloe was *crying* – oh God, this was going to take for ever. When your best mate rings you up in tears, you don't say, *'This isn't a very convenient time . . . can I call you back?'*, do you?

'Hey, Chloe, babe, cheer up!' I had to overwhelm her with forgiveness and make things better immediately, even though she had said my ears were weird.

'No! No! I was horrible to you, Zoe! I said bitchy things and I didn't mean them! I was stupid! I asked you to go through my wardrobe and then when you did I got touchy! I'm so sorry!'

'Don't worry, Chloe!' I insisted. 'It was nothing!'

'I'm so so sorry, Zoe! Please forgive me!'

'There's absolutely *nothing* to forgive! I've forgotten all about it!' This was true – but only because, since I'd got home, worse torments had unfolded. 'Listen – you were right about my ears. I'm going to get a pair of Hallowe'en goblin ears to wear instead!' This was supposed to be a joke to cheer her up, but it set off another great storm of crying.

'Chloe, Chloe . . .' I persisted gently. 'Stop it, this is boring! It is so not necessary! I haven't even thought about it since I got home! It was my fault anyway. I should never have stamped off like that. It was stupid.'

'Your ears are lovely! I like your ears! They're cute!'

'Look, let's just shut up about my ears, shall we? When are you coming round to tell me my clothes are crap?'

'I'm not! I'm not! It's too mean! It'll destroy our relationship! Anyway, your clothes are cool!' I was secretly satisfied by this little victory.

'OK, OK.' I tried not to sound too hasty, even though I was longing to end the call and get back to Beast, because I had to put him straight about the mythical Dan. 'Let's forget all about it, OK? Love you! See you tomorrow!'

'Wait! Wait, Zoe!' It was like being caught on barbed wire. Poor Chloe had no idea how irritating she was being, and it was totally not her fault because, of course, she was acting as nice as pie. 'Listen! We've got to start this aerobics thing – and guess what!'

'What? What?' I tried to sound intensely inter-ested, even though I was desperate to end the call.

'Guess what! I've ordered a hip-hop exercise DVD!'

'Awesome! Sounds great! I can't wait to hop my hips! See you in the morning!'

'No, Zoe, wait! I need to ask you something!'

Though tempted to hurl my mobile out of the window, I confined myself to secretly jumping up and down in an anguished manner and irritably flapping my free hand as if Chloe was a persistent wasp. My wardrobe shook.

'What?'

'The history homework . . .' My heart sank. It was no use Chloe asking me about history homework. I literally hadn't given it a thought since I'd had to do the last lot of history homework, and to be honest, scarcely even then. 'It has to be in by tomorrow, right?'

'I don't know. Probably.' I began to feel tormented from an entirely new angle. A history essay had to be cooked up somehow before tomorrow morning without any preparation whatsoever. Thank God Tam was at home, because I was going to have to steal her university brain – just for half an hour.

'Oh, and I've had one more idea for our makeover programme . . .' Chloe went on.

Suddenly, to my horror, I heard Tam's bedroom door open. She said goodbye to Beast, and then there was the sound of his footsteps going downstairs. I was mesmerised by those footsteps, distraught at the thought that Beast had left without even saying goodbye to me, and worst of all, I was in despair that he still thought I was mad about somebody called Dan. I wallowed in agony for a couple of moments, deaf to every word Chloe was saying.

'. . . if that's OK?' she concluded.

'Fine,' I agreed absently, not listening.

'And we start tomorrow?'

'Sure.' I just wanted to end the call, now. I wasn't even listening to what *I* was saying, let alone Chloe.

'See you tomorrow, then, Zoe. You're the best mate in the history of the universe!'

'Only the universe?' I quipped. 'You're always so hard on people!'

Chloe laughed and rang off. I sat, exhausted, on the bed for a moment, then went back into Tam's room. She was at the mirror, doing her eye make-up.

'Typical of bloody Beast to turn up without giving me a chance to do my eyes!' she grumbled. Tam had spent five minutes in Beast's company and hugged him and she hadn't even realised how lucky she was.

'What difference does it make anyway?' I asked. 'You don't even fancy him.'

There was a horrible sickening pause while Tam stood and thought about it. My heart plummeted. My stomach rioted. My legs jellified. I uttered a swift silent prayer to all the gods that my sister wouldn't fancy Beast, because if she did, she'd be sure to sweep him off his feet with her wit and beauty, and I'd end up being the ugly tortured bridesmaid to the man I adored.

Still, it would make a great screenplay, and it would have a fabulous unexpected ending in which I would get very rich and have a posh house in London and refuse to invite them to any of my parties. Beast would realise after a while that Tam was not the sister he really loved, and he would start to send me letters blotted with tears, telling me how mad he was about me, and imploring me to let him have a lock of my hair. And I would tell the butler to send Beast a lock of the dog's hair (a Pekinese, naturally).

'No, I don't think I really fancy Beast,' said Tam. 'He's too *obviously* attractive, don't you think?'

'Yeah, I guess,' I agreed. Although cross with Tam for dissing Beast, I was also relieved that she didn't fancy him. 'You look gorgeous anyway,' I said. 'You always do.' I went over to give her a hug. Everything I'd said was true, but I also wanted to soften her up because later I was going to ask her to help me with my history essay.

And who knows, there might still be a whiff of Beast's aftershave clinging to her, following their recent hug. When you're a victim of unrequited love you have to make do with leftovers. I launched myself into her arms, but was disappointed to find that she was only covered from head to foot in her own Jean Paul Gaultier.

Chapter 7

I arrived at school early next day and was grabbed by my dearest male buddy, Toby.

'Listen, Zoe Morris, you animal!' said Toby urgently. 'Did you do the history essay? And if so, please may I copy large chunks of it in exchange for as many sweets as you can eat?' Toby has size issues, a bit like me, but in his case sugar is his downfall. He orders retro sweeties from a website. 'I've got sherbet lemons!' hissed Tobe. 'I've got chocolate tools! I've got bonbons! I've got giant white jazzles! Name your fave item and it's yours in bulk!'

'Listen, you weirdo, I'll be the bulk item if I give in to your devilish temptation!' I retorted sternly, handing over my history folder. 'You can copy the essay, sure, and the good news is, Tam's home, so it's five-star egghead stuff. Watch out! You may win the Nobel Prize.'

'Don't worry!' beamed Toby. 'I'll only use bits of it and I'll string it together with some drivel of my own so Hughesie will never suspect! I'll go and do it in the cloakroom, OK? See you at registration. And I owe you, big time!'

Tobe minced swiftly off, and I whipped out my mirror and checked my face. Nigel, my prize zit, was surfacing on my chin like some kind of extra-terrestrial alien parasite. Maybe Toby's mention of giant white jazzles had roused Nigel from his slumber.

'Get lost, Nigel!' I snapped.

Suddenly Jess Jordan appeared beside me, accompanied by her faithful boyfriend Fred Parsons. Jess is short and dark with crazy eyebrows and a cute buzzy kind of voice, and Fred is a long gangling guy with a kind of limp ironic style. They write and perform funny scripts – they're going to be the next big thing – and they'd got a comedy sketch spot in Jailhouse Rock, between acts, so this was a chance for me to lead the conversation in a Beastly direction.

'So how's the sketch going?' I asked. 'For Jailhouse Rock?'

'We've been through, like, a thousand different sketches,' groaned Jess.

'My favourite was the one about argumentative fruit,' sighed Fred. 'And then there were the twins in the womb . . . the computer viruses were kind of cool, too . . . but we think we've finally got it sorted. It's about –'

'Shut up, Fred!' shouted Jess, slamming her hand across his mouth. 'We mustn't tell anybody, remember? Or it'll ruin it! It's got to stay a secret till the big night. God! I'm so nervous, though. Imagine the size of the audience! Plunkett is immense!'

'Beast seems a bit stressed about the organisation,' I said, trying to pronounce the sacred B-word without flinching.

'Oh yeah, poor old Beast is tearing his hair out. We're all going to rally round though, when the posters and handouts and stuff are ready. We'll be tramping the streets. Beast's got this plan to leaflet every house in the city!'

'What?' I pricked up my ears. Beast's ambitious plan was going to need an army of helpers. I was determined that, somehow or other, I would be there for him, Chloe or no Chloe.

'But the worst thing, kind of,' Jess went on, 'Beast's

real nightmare is that Rose Quartz might not turn up. She agreed to come and now she's playing hard to get.'

'Of course she'll come! I mean, it's for charity and everything!' I insisted, talking from my deep knowledge of nothing at all.

'Do you think we'll get to meet her? Yessssss! Yay!!!!!' Jess grabbed Fred's sleeve and squealed in an ecstasy of excitement. Fred just cringed.

'I hope not,' he shuddered. 'I would faint with terror.'

At this point Chloe appeared beside me. 'Hi, guys!' she grinned. 'Come on, then, Zoe. We've just got time.'

'Just got time for what?' I asked.

'Come on! We run once round the school field before registration, remember? Our exercise programme – you promised!'

A horrible realisation crept over me: I remembered Chloe going on about something yesterday, when she'd phoned in the middle of Beast's visit to our house, and I'd been so tormented by the sound of his footsteps going downstairs that I hadn't been able to concentrate on what she was saying. Evidently I'd agreed to some kind of frightful physical ordeal involving running – an activity God did not have in mind when he designed my podgy knock-kneed bod.

'Come on!' Chloe cruelly grabbed a handful of flab on my right hip and squeezed so hard it hurt. 'We'll soon get rid of this! There's just time! Hey, Jess, hold our bags, will you?'

Before I knew what had happened, Chloe had separated me from my bag and dragged me off round the school field. I realised it was too late to argue, and as I am just a tad overweight, maybe this was a good idea after all. I broke into what I hoped was a cool stylish trot, although, worryingly, I could feel my upper arms kind of *jingling* at every step.

By the time we were halfway round, I was gasping like a goldfish out of water, my thighs were whacking against each other at every stride, and my bra had gone limp with the effort of containing my flying fandangos. Sweat was pumping from my armpits and the air was burning in my throat. I was never going to be transformed into a goddess in seven days. It would take seven years to burn off all those slabs of lard. Chloe had practically disappeared into the distance – her skinny little frame is perfect for long-distance running, and disastrously, I could hear the faraway sound of the bell ringing for registration, so slowing to a dignified walk wasn't an option. I had, if anything, to accelerate in order to avoid the wrath of Mrs Young, our form teacher.

I arrived in the form room bright red in the face and wheezing like an ancient church organ with a puncture. Chloe had collected our bags from Jess and arrived before me.

'Zoe!?' Mrs Young looked up quizzically. 'What's this? Training for the marathon?'

'Chloe and I –' I gasped, 'are – working on our – fitness.'

'Sit down,' said Mrs Young. 'And do try and keep the noise down. There's nothing I hate more first thing in the morning than the sound of rasping lungs.'

I fell into a chair beside Chloe, who was also panting, but slightly less hysterically, and as I sat down she patted my thigh in congratulation. Toby looked across from his table and gave me the thumbs up. Evidently the history essay had been taken care of.

I sat still, closed my eyes and waited for my heart to slow and my breathing to return to normal. But gradually, I became aware of something quite frightful: slowly, stealthily, something was creeping up my neck and enveloping my nostrils. It was the smell of sweat.

And when I say sweat, I don't mean the fragrant dew of roses and lilies that adorns the flesh of goddesses. I'm talking soup – I'm talking *onion* soup, made with the freshest, pongiest onions, highlighted with a hint of garlic and burning with a dash of chilli. Though the smell of onion soup can be delicious – Dad makes a mean one, and the aroma has lured me down from my bedroom many a time – it's not really the sort of smell one would wish to have coming from one's *armpits*.

Oh God! I was seriously pongy and first lesson was double English with Mr Fawcett, our new, slightly camp, rather delightful teacher. Though I hadn't got a crush on him or anything extreme like that, I would hate him to find me unfragrant, because he himself is always one hundred per cent sniffable – mainly Ralph Lauren's *Explorer* ('notes of Sicilian bergamot, Russian coriander and Australian sandalwood . . . for the man who lives his life without limits'). It's true that Ashcroft School is a wild and challenging place where feral creatures roam, and perhaps *Explorer* made Mr Fawcett feel a little bit more confident. Nothing is worse than realising that you stink. I clamped my arms as tightly as possible to my sides and whispered to Chloe.

'Have you got any deodorant on you?'

Chloe looked alarmed and shook her head, swiftly opened her blazer and sniffed her own armpits, then pulled a hideous face and slammed her blazer shut. It seemed that our plan to become goddesses would have to be put on hold whilst we struggled not to become hobos.

Chapter 8

Nobody in our class had deodorant with them at school. Nobody! We raced to the loos – we had just a few moments before first lesson to try and banish our stench.

'Quick! Quick! Who's got deodorant?' yelled Chloe at the gang of girls milling about by the loos. Daisy 'Pooch' Archer and Emily 'Titch' Langham were using the drinking fountain. They looked startled. 'Perfume? Anything!' demanded Chloe.

'I've got some scent,' said Pooch doubtfully, rummaging in her bag. She has long wavy hanks of chestnut hair hanging down on either side of her face which makes her look slightly like a spaniel.

'Quick! Quick!' shouted Chloe, ripping off her blazer and undoing her shirt. 'Just a quick squirt! I'll pay you!' Pooch held out the spray. It was a cheap one I'd rejected last year because though it did have a cheerful citrus twang, it also came with a tea-tree overload, a bit too close to the smell of loo cleaner.

'Chloe!' I couldn't diss Pooch's scent, but maybe I could make Chloe think twice. 'We should wash our armpits first!' I was struggling with my own shirt buttons. I managed to get one arm out.

'No time! No time!' jabbered Chloe, grabbing the scent spray and giving herself a double blast in each armpit, inside her open shirt. Then she offered the scent to me.

'No, thanks!' I felt flustered. A still, small voice inside my head suggested that even real loo cleaner would be preferable to the kind of onion soup I was currently pumping out, but I was still hoping to achieve a clean hygienic effect by that good old-fashioned technique known as washing.

'Come on, Pooch!' urged Titch. 'We mustn't be late for Powell!'

'Oh no!' gasped Pooch, grabbing her scent and heading for the door.

The bell for first lesson shredded the air with deaf-ening noise, so our double English with Mr Fawcett was seconds away, but I had only just managed to make one of the taps work. Pooch and Titch disappeared into the hurly-burly of the corridor. I raced up and down the washbasins trying to find a liquid soap dispenser that hadn't run out. The school loos were such crap! My left arm was still outside my shirt, and a powerful stink of onion soup followed me up and down.

'Ow! Ouch! Aaargh!' yelled Chloe, as I gave up on soap and scooped a handful of icy water on to my left pit, and rubbed. 'That goddam scent is stinging!' shrieked Chloe. 'It's a killer! Oooooourgh! My armpits are on fire!' She flapped her arms up and down like a baby bird trying to fly, and then thrust her fists into her armpits and winced for England.

I was discovering that water on its own is no good: soap and a flannel are essential to human happiness. I would never leave home without them in future. My handful of cold water had done nothing for the stinkiness of my armpit – it had merely soaked the left-hand side of my shirt and spread the onion soup smell about even more. Hastily I buttoned up again.

'Help! God! Please, God, make my armpits stop stinging!' begged Chloe as we raced towards English.

'I think God may have more pressing crises to attend to,' I gasped, 'but, hey! If not – please, God, remove my terrible pong!'

'I'm allergic to this goddam scent!' screeched Chloe. 'My armpits are literally *killing me!*'

We arrived apologetically just as Mr Fawcett was giving some books out. I was holding my arms as close to my body as a peg doll at a car boot sale, and Chloe was pale and hysterical with suppressed stinging. We joined Toby and Fergus at a table by the window.

'OK, uhhhh.' Mr Fawcett handed us a couple of books, and a divine gust of Ralph Lauren's *Explorer* washed over us. I was so tempted to ask if he had it with him and if I could borrow a blast, but I'm not that cheeky.

'Settle down now!' said Mr Fawcett. 'We're going to read a really mysterious poem today, by William Blake. Find page fifty-six.'

'Hi, girls!' whispered Tobe. His breath smelt of chocolate. He slid my history file along to me. 'I owe you!' He winked, giving his signature thumbs up.

Suddenly I had a mad, but possibly brilliant idea. Mr Fawcett was eyeing us critically, so I found page fifty-six and tried to look studious and grand, whilst holding my armpits firmly shut. My brilliant idea would have to wait for Mr Fawcett to look elsewhere.

'Blake lived in London and produced his best poetry between about 1780 and 1820, so two hundred years ago,' said Mr Fawcett. I looked up eagerly and nodded, maintaining contact with his sweet pale-blue eyes. 'He was quite an – er, eccentric person. In fact, some people thought he was mad. He had visions.' Mr Fawcett looked anxiously towards George Flint and Seth Mortimer, who were sitting in the opposite corner and making a bit of a noise. I felt I could rely on them to provide me with cover.

'I just saw Ben Jones in his football gear!' whispered Toby.

'Never mind Ben Jones!' I whispered back – the first and only time I would dismiss BJ as a topic of conversation. 'Hand over your sweeties!'

Toby got a huge bag of sweets out of his bag and secretly passed them along to me under the table. I coughed to cover the sound of the paper crackling open, and peeped inside – whilst pretending to look at the open poetry book. Mr Fawcett was starting to read.

'*O Rose, thou art sick* . . .' he intoned in his special camp poetry voice.

'Please, sir!' interrupted Flinters. 'Is this about Rose Davis in Year 10? She was sick on the school trip!' Everybody giggled. I felt a bit sorry for Mr Fawcett, but I didn't have time to sympathise with him now. Fergus was sniffing the air.

'IThinkIt'sOnionSoupForLunchToday!' he whispered. He talks like that, all in a rush. 'OrMaybeHamburgersWithFriedOnions!' Oh no. Fergus could smell my sweat and he was literally five feet away – sitting at the other side of our table! I cringed and tried to rein in my sweating by sheer will power whilst examining Toby's huge collection of sweeties. There had to be some here that were suitable. I was going to reinvent sweets as an alternative form of deodorant. Brilliant, huh?

Obviously boiled sweets were out, because they'd be sticky, and chocolate was out, because it would be messy. I needed something light-coloured but the same kind of texture as chocolate, like a kind of solid perfume.

'It's not about a specific person,' explained Mr Fawcett, ignoring Flinters's wisecrack. 'It's about a rose, although the rose might symbolise something.' I hoped for Mr Fawcett's sake there weren't any other iffy words in this poem, because Flinters was in the mood for fun.

Ah! I found the perfect sweet. It was white and

shaped like a disc. There were several of them. In a few moments I was hoping to replace onion soup with the scent of white chocolate. Who knows? I could be on the brink of a major cosmetics breakthrough.

Furtively I undid the middle couple of buttons on my shirt, while Mr Fawcett read on.

'*The invisible worm*
That flies in the night . . .'

I lifted the white disc to my lips. I reckoned I had to moisten it first, to help the smearing process. The disc was hidden in my hand. I pretended to rest my chin on my hand, and secretly licked the disc when I knew Mr Fawcett wasn't looking. Then, very slowly and quietly, I sneaked the disc inside my shirt and smeared and squidged it about inside my armpit.

'*In the howling storm . . .*' Mr Fawcett went on fragrantly.

Flinters interrupted again, 'Sir, what's the invisible worm?'

'Let's just get to the end of the poem before we try to work out what it means,' insisted Mr Fawcett patiently. No teacher had ever allowed us to interrupt an actual poem being read before. Mr Fawcett was such a wuss. But he had managed to maintain some kind of discipline right at the start of term by sending Seth and Flinters to Mr Powell (Irritable Powell – Deputy Head and fearsome roaring lion).

He looked round the class for support and response. I nodded understandingly, even though I was halfway through removing my hand from my shirt. I pretended I was adjusting my bra. Mr Fawcett looked embarrassed and went back to his book.

'Has found out thy bed
Of crimson joy . . .'

'Please, sir, is that rude?' Flinters again.

Oh my God! I'd finally got my hand out of my shirt and my fingers were covered in chocolate – and I mean *brown* chocolate! The whiteness of the disc had apparently only been a kind of coating. I had smeared brown goo all over my right armpit and by now it must be all over my shirt, too!

'Just let's read the poem through first, George, so we get a sense of it as a whole,' snapped Mr Fawcett irritably.

'A hole, sir?' Flinters sniggered. Mr Fawcett looked exasperated. Hastily and secretly I licked my fingers. I had no hankie and no tissues. I would never come to school so badly equipped again. How was I going to repair the damage to my ghastly, smeary, hideously chocolatey armpit?

'And his dark secret love
Does thy life destroy.'

Mr Fawcett had finished. It was quite a short poem, thank God. Although weird.

There was an explosion of sniggering from Flinters's table, and while Mr Fawcett was distracted, I managed to bend down and whip a panty liner out of my bag, unwrap it and smuggle it swiftly inside my shirt.

'What's Blake trying to describe here?' appealed Mr Fawcett, going red in the face.

'Please, sir,' said Monkey Hatton, 'it could be, like, aphids, you know – er, greenfly.' Several of the girls screamed slightly, as insects had been mentioned. I would have screamed myself if I hadn't been so busy secretly sticking a panty liner to my armpit. 'My nan sprays her roses,' added Monkey helpfully.

'Well, you could be on the right lines, in a way,' nodded Mr Fawcett. I nodded, too, partly in relief. I had managed to secure the panty liner to the inside of my shirt. So at least one armpit was now smelling slightly less of onions and slightly more of chocolate, even if the other one was still not only oniony but uncomfortably wet. Still, my crisis was nothing compared to the bad morning Mr Fawcett was having.

'Although the poem seems to be about a rose and a worm, what I'm asking you to think about is what might those things *symbolise*?'

'My pits are going to need surgery!' growled Chloe in agony, her fists still plunged deeply into her stinging armpits. 'Skin grafts off my bum! The only hope!'

After English, Mr Fawcett limped off towards the staff room leaving a wonderful waft of Ralph Lauren. We headed for the loos. We now had the whole of break to deal with our vandalised armpits. We were whimpering hysterically as we charged along the corridor: Chloe was still in pain, but my own anguish was mostly mental.

'Gaaaaaad!' I groaned. 'What a nightmare! How could things possibly get worse?!?!'

Just then Ben Jones and Tim Huddlestone came round the corner and walked towards us in their football shorts: normally this would be an opportunity for some appreciative drooling and eyeballing (on our part, naturally), but right now we were almost too traumatised to bother. As we drew level with them, however, Tim locked eyes with me and said, 'Uh, I think – you dropped something . . . ?'

I followed his gaze, turned around and saw, to my complete and utter horror, the panty liner! Which had fallen out of my armpit and *lay behind me on the floor*, liberally adorned with melted chocolate!

'It's only chocolate!' I yelled, diving down and snatching it up into my bag, then tried to perform a wacky grin, as if it was all a riotous joke we'd deliberately staged, and ran off towards the loos. Well, towards South America, actually, which is where I'm planning to hide until I'm about fifty-seven. I'm sure, if I live to be a hundred, I'll never suffer a moment of greater horror and embarrassment.

Chapter 9

We were a million miles away from being even very minor goddesses; in fact, our efforts so far had only led to us falling right down the food chain and acquiring the charisma of tiny slimy things that live in ponds.

Two days later the hip-hop DVD arrived, so Chloe and I started on our aerobic workouts. It was great, even though I was panting like a hippo after only two minutes. As I walked home, I thought about other ways to get fit. Delivering leaflets was an obvious possibility. Mum says walking is the best exercise, and she and Dad sometimes go on walking holidays and take heroic photos of themselves being blasted by gales on mountaintops.

Walking around town delivering Beast's leaflets

wasn't so melodramatic, but it could certainly turn out to be romantic, as long as I could keep clear of Matthew and somehow keep seeing Beast. '*Uhhh, Beastie darling,*' I would murmur, '*could you just take me through the business of putting a leaflet through a letter box? I'm not quite sure how to do it.*' And he'd stand behind me sort of cuddling up against my back and talking me through the whole thing, but somehow, you know, I still wouldn't get it, and he'd have to give me private lessons for hours and hours.

Helping to publicise Jailhouse Rock would be brilliant for two main reasons: I'd have an excuse to see Beast and I'd burn off a few calories. The only problem was Chloe. It was so tricky trying to get involved with something behind her back.

Of course I should have sat down with her and said, '*Look here, Chloe, you may not want to help with Jailhouse Rock, but I do, and I'm going to.*' If it was just a question of wanting to help, really, it would have been straightforward. But it wasn't just a question of wanting to help. It was, of course, a question of wanting to see Beast – just see him, quietly, in a room full of other people if necessary. He didn't even have to speak to me. Well, ultimately it was a question of me being mad about Beast, and Chloe having recently been mad about Beast. Dodgy territory.

I tried to compose a text to Beast offering to help, but it was too much of a challenge trying to make it sound glamorous, sexy, casual, cool, generous, delightful, witty and irresistible, and still convey the essential information. I decided that instead of sending him a text, I would casually drop into the Major Events office on Saturday morning, see him in person and offer to help. I couldn't go before Saturday because I didn't want Beast to see me in school uniform.

For the rest of the week, Chloe was busy every evening with her family, because her dad had come home from Dubai. Whenever this happens, her mum Fran organises lots of events so people can see him and hear all about his glamorous life in Dubai. I think she likes to prove to people that he's still around. Chloe went a bit quiet at school – she was tired, trying to fit in homework with all of her social obligations. Our self-improvement project had to go on the back burner for a bit.

'I can't do the hip-hop routine,' she grumbled, 'because my dad won't let me play loud music or anything. We're never going to be goddesses in seven days.'

'Well, twenty-seven days, then,' I suggested. 'Or something like that. Rome wasn't built in a day.' Chloe looked relieved. I felt relieved myself. We'd set ourselves an impossible task with that seven days idea.

'Shall we give up on the seven days schedule, then?' asked Chloe. 'But still stay on track to be goddesses, right?'

'Right!' I agreed. 'Gimme a high five! Goddesses by – well . . .'

'Goddesses ASAP!' giggled Chloe. Thank God that little bit of pressure was off. There was enough stress to deal with in everyday life.

Friday came, and I was beginning to get nervous about dropping in at Beast's office the next morning.

'Hey, Zoe!' said Chloe. 'My parents are going away together this weekend. They'll be away till Sunday. So is it OK if I come round yours on Saturday night?'

'Yeah, sure,' I said. 'My parents will be away, too: they're doing some kind of walking weekend in the Peak District.'

'Wow!' grinned Chloe. 'Let's throw a party and wreck the joint!'

'Great idea!' I agreed. 'And then we can throw

another one at your place and wreck that, too.'

'Let's meet in the morning in town!' suggested Chloe. 'Then we can decide which goddess frocks we're going to get for Jailhouse Rock!'

'We mustn't make it too early,' I warned her anxiously. I needed to keep the morning free for my visit to Beast's office. 'Let's say twelve. After all, it is Saturday. I need my beauty sleep.'

'OK,' agreed Chloe. 'I'll see you by the town hall at noon. You'll recognise me because I'll be wearing one of my stylish coats made of Weetabix and dead rats.'

All Friday evening I planned what I was going to wear when I dropped in at the Major Events office the next morning. I had to look glamorous, sexy, casual, cool, generous, delightful, witty and irresistible. But in an effortless kind of way – not as if I'd had to work hard at it, but because I was just naturally overflowing with all those things.

I glared into my wardrobe. Though quieter than Chloe's, it was still a disappointment. Nothing in there was quite right for a Saturday morning in town. I am at my best dressed up for a night out. But I could hardly teeter into the Major Events office in killer leopard-print heels and a pink minidress, could I?

My daytime casual clothes really did need an overhaul. Because Tam had gone back to uni, I had a quick flick through her wardrobe, but the best stuff was gone and the only things hanging there were a few boho items left over from her recent phase, all lace and batik and fussy stuff. I am so not boho. I would almost rather be hobo than boho.

Next morning Mum and Dad were up early, getting ready to leave for the Peak District. They were going to stay the night at a little B&B beside a stream, and Mum was pleased I'd invited Chloe to spend the night so I wouldn't be Home Alone.

'No drugs,' she said sternly, cleaning her shoes. 'No drink, no sex.'

'Well, that may be your plan for the weekend,' I smiled cheekily, 'but Chloe and I are throwing a party here and inviting two thousand people off the Internet.'

Mum went pale. 'Don't even joke about that sort of stuff, Zoe,' she murmured, giving me a long hard look as if she knew it was just a joke, but the thought of it had made her feel quite ill.

Once they'd gone, first of all I applied six layers of deodorant. I wasn't going to make that mistake again. Onion soup must be banished for ever. I decided to wear skinny jeans and a star-print hoodie. It looked OK, but I'd been too nervous to eat much breakfast and I was afraid my breath would smell. I chewed some parsley (Dad taught me that little trick – apparently he used to chew parsley when he was a teenager so his mum and dad wouldn't know when he'd been smoking or drinking). Then I chewed some gum.

I spent one thousand years on my make-up – I actually took the whole lot off twice and started over again. I wasn't sure whether Beast liked girls wearing make-up. Boys are a bit weird about cosmetics: they don't see the point. I am of course *obsessed* with make-up, so what boys think is irrelevant, even Beast. I mean, I'm prepared to make some concessions to impress the opposite sex. If Beast required me to go to Africa and wrestle lions single-handedly, that would be no problem. But he'd have to accept that I would need to spend an hour on lion-proof mascara and safari lipgloss, first.

Eventually I was ready. I wore a pair of flat shoes to show that I wasn't some kind of teetering ninny, although I didn't rule it out as a stylish career option at some point in the future. With my sturdy flat shoes I would be fine trudging up and down the city streets delivering Beast's leaflets.

I walked up and down the high street twice, right past his office, before I plucked up the courage to go in. Major Events is above an employment agency; I went up the stairs and found myself in reception. A bored-looking girl looked up. How could she be bored with Beast working there?

'Hi,' I wheezed, trying to sound charismatic but instead sounding asthmatic. 'I've come to see Harry Hawkins about Jailhouse Rock.'

'Up to the top.' The girl pointed to the ceiling with her pen. 'Turn left at the top of the stairs, and it's right at the end of the corridor.'

I went up more stairs, puffing and panting. I had to get fit. I was going to have to up my hip-hop routine to twice a day. This was ridiculous. I didn't want Beast to think I was a feeble lardass – although in fact, that's exactly what I am. He, of course, is the captain of a local rugby team called the Antelopes, and last year he was the rugby megastar of Ashcroft School, so he is uber-fit – in both senses of the word.

I found myself outside a door with a handwritten sign taped to it which said *JAILHOUSE ROCK*. I knocked, my heart thudding with uncontrollable love and unaccustomed exercise.

'Come in!' called a girl's voice. Sickened by the sound, I pushed my way in and found myself face to face with Charlie. It was a small office with two desks. She was sitting at the smaller one. The larger one was empty.

'Oh, hi, Charlie!' I said. She looked blank for a moment.

'Oh, hey, great to see you!' she said, smiling, after a tiny hesitation. 'God, I'm so sorry, I've forgotten your name. I'm so hopeless with names, it's a disaster. Was it Leonie?'

'Zoe,' I said. 'Is . . . Beast around?'

'He's in a meeting with my uncle,' said Charlie. 'Can I help?'

My heart sank. I had spent the last twelve hours preparing myself mentally, physically, emotionally and style-wise for this moment, and it had been a complete waste of time.

'I just thought I might be able to spare a bit of time to help,' I said. 'Poor Beast! He looked so stressed out. It must be a nightmare for him.'

'You know Beast quite well, don't you?' asked Charlie with a thoughtful and, to be honest, rather calculating little smile.

'Well, you know . . .' I shrugged. 'A little . . .

Newquay, last summer . . .' I let it hang in the air, as if Beast and I had been sitting on the beach until dawn every night for a week. If only.

'Tell you what,' said Charlie, getting up and diving into her jacket. 'Let's grab a coffee, shall we? Have you got time? Then I could fill you in on what we've been doing so far.'

I assumed this was to do with Jailhouse Rock rather than what she and Beast might be getting up to in their leisure moments. But to be honest, dedicated though I was to supporting Amnesty International, it was the personal stuff I was really interested in.

As we reached the street, Charlie plucked at the sleeve of my hoodie.

'Great top,' she said. 'Where did you get it?'

'Charity shop,' I lied. I had decided not to play competitive games with her. In fact, I was going to play a private game of my own. Then she did something really strange. She linked arms with me as we walked off, as if we'd been best mates all our lives. And this was a girl who, three minutes ago, hadn't even been able to remember my name.

'So,' she whispered confidentially, 'when did you first meet the mysterious Mr Hawkins?' And she followed it up with a giggle which I didn't quite like.

'Oh, God knows,' I sighed, as if I couldn't be less interested. 'I've known Beast, uhhh, for ever.'

Chapter 10

We went to the Dolphin Cafe. Charlie got an espresso and I chose a chai latte. I was guilty about how many calories I was going to be sipping, but I had a feeling I'd need a bit of strength to cope with this conversation and I hadn't been able to have much breakfast because I'd been too excited, thinking I'd be seeing Beast. My three different layers of lipgloss were going to be wasted on Charlie. At the last minute, approaching the till, I gave in to temptation and grabbed a croissant.

'So,' said Charlie, flaring her eyes across the table with a questioning smile. I had to admire her mascara. 'You'd like to help?'

'Yes,' I said. 'I mean, I couldn't do much, because of school, but I could manage a few hours a week.

What sort of help does Beast need?'

'Well, he does have a full-time PA,' giggled Charlie. 'That's *moi*, obviously, although I'm not really paid – well, it's peanuts, but of course it's for charity, and it's my gap year, and it'll look great on my CV so . . . no worries.'

I was somehow already rather irritated with her and I had a feeling things could only get worse.

'I got the impression that people were letting him down?' I asked.

'Well, there has been a bit of that,' said Charlie. 'Paolo – that's your friend, isn't it?'

'Well, Matthew, actually, and he's not really a friend,' I explained hastily. 'He wanted a life coach, once, ages ago and I – we – kind of gave him a couple of sessions.'

'Oh! So it was your idea that he change his name to Paolo?'

'No way!' I tried to smile, although I was already clearly losing the conversation on points. 'He was always going on about changing his name to Brad. I advised him not to.' I pursed my lips. I had gone into headmistress mode. I do that sometimes – it's a reaction to stress. 'I was just trying to train him to shake hands and smile – and that was a mountain to climb.

91

Oh, and I advised him to wear brown.'

'Brown?' exclaimed Charlie, raising a beautifully plucked eyebrow and sounding surprised in a way which seemed rather rude. 'Why brown?' She was questioning my style advice. I wanted to put her down. But I couldn't be too prickly and defensive, because I needed her to open up to me about Beast.

'Oh, I can't remember what I said to Matthew,' I said, trying for a glamorous, irresponsible grin. 'I just used to say the first thing that came into my head. The whole thing was kind of a piss-take, anyway. His eyes are brown, as I recall. Or khaki, in fact. It's not a colour one sees much on Planet Earth.'

'I love brown eyes!' sighed Charlie. 'But grey-green ones are even better.' I just knew she was thinking of Beast. Her eyes were blue with tiny black flecks, a bit like beautiful birds' eggs. I envied her deeply and could only assume that Beast had noticed her eyes and been impressed.

'Anyway . . . Matthew's helping with publicity?' I asked, wanting to steer the conversation away from grey-green eyes as a feeling of jealous weakness had come over me.

'Yes, in theory, although every time we recruit

92

somebody new to his team, somebody else seems to drop out.'

'Maybe Matthew's putting them off.'

'That had occurred to us,' said Charlie with a sigh. Then she gave me a cheeky little look. 'I don't think you made much progress with your life coaching, Zoe!' She giggled. 'Maybe Matthew should ask for his money back!' Though this was obviously a joke, I was starting to want to kick her.

'He never paid, in fact,' I admitted, as if I didn't care.

'What? You didn't invoice him?' Charlie's well-shaped eyebrows shot up. I was beginning to feel claustrophobic. I had to get rid of Matthew as a subject of conversation. He could only drag me down and make me seem like some sad trashy loser.

'It was so informal . . .' I drawled, staring out of the window at a toddler having a tantrum outside a newsagent. I wanted to have a tantrum myself. 'Anyway . . . forget Matthew. What can I do to help?'

'Oh, there are loads of things,' said Charlie. 'But nothing glamorous. It's mostly leafleting, I'm afraid. We need an army of people just basically pavement-bashing, as soon as we get the posters and leaflets printed.'

'When will that be?'

'Well, I've busted a gut over the poster competition,' Charlie said proudly. 'When I get a bee in my bonnet about something, I really kick ass!' For a moment a strange image flashed up in my mind, of bees wearing bonnets and kicking asses. 'I'm just like that – people say I'm crazy, nobody really understands me, but I can't help myself, that's the way I am!' Charlie smiled broadly. She was so up herself.

'We've had loads of entries in the competition,' she went on, 'due largely to my mum who's a primary school teacher. It's terribly last-minute so a lot of schools just couldn't participate. But we've already got enough entries to make it a proper competition and we're drawing up a shortlist. We'll be choosing the winner on Wednesday and with any luck we'll be able to start leafleting the week after – if the printer doesn't let us down.'

'Great,' I nodded. 'Beast seemed very stressed out about it.'

'Yeah . . .' A strange look came into Charlie's eyes. 'You know the amazing Beast, right? When did you meet?' She seemed determined to interrogate me. Her eyes raced around my face for clues about my relationship with Beast.

'Oh, ages ago,' I said. 'He was always a bit of a legend at school, you know. And my sister Tam – she's at uni now – she knows him quite well. In fact he saved her life in Newquay last summer.'

'What? Like, swimming?' asked Charlie, her eyes huge with surprise.

'No,' I explained. 'Tam had appendicitis and Beast was the only person who realised how ill she was. He rang the ambulance and went to hospital with her and everything.'

'Oh my God, how amazing!' exclaimed Charlie. 'He is going to be a doctor, though, so no wonder he was on the ball. I think I might be a doctor myself. Or a physio. People have said I've got a healing presence. Apparently my aura is deep green.'

'Really?' I said, trying not to sound faintly disgusted.

'Between you and me, I'm not sure Beast is completely committed to medicine as a career, though,' said Charlie. 'He was telling me the other day that he quite fancied something a bit more adventurous – zoology, maybe. He opens up to me for some reason – I get the feeling he hasn't really got anybody to talk to. And I'm a good listener. Let me give you this little piece of advice, Zoe – it's one of my grandma's

95

little sayings: *keep your ears open and your mouth shut.* She has a lot of insight and I seem to have inherited it.'

This advice was ironical, coming from a girl who apparently never stopped boasting about herself. I was furious that she'd implied Beast only confided in her, and felt jealous of all the long hours they were spending together in that office, whereas I had to plot and plan just to arrange a glimpse of him.

'Well,' I shrugged, 'I don't suppose Beast will have a career organising events. Although he is brilliant at it.'

'Well . . . sort of!' Charlie produced a kind of irritating giggle. 'He's so absent-minded and disorganised. If it wasn't for me he'd have got into big trouble with the directors last week. He lost a report and forgot a meeting.'

'Well, brilliant of you to rescue him,' I said with deepest sarcasm, though trying to conceal it as genuine admiration.

'Poor Beast,' said Charlie, laughing to herself as if remembering the many scrapes she had rescued him from. 'He is so lovely, though, bless him.'

I suddenly felt faint and bit into my croissant. One thousand croissant crumbs instantly got stuck to my three layers of lipgloss. I tried to capture them with my teeth in a series of lip-scraping forays which must have looked truly gross.

'Tell me, Zoe,' Charlie lowered her voice, 'were Beast and your sister ever . . . an item?'

'No,' I said, flakily. 'Why?'

'Oh, I don't know. He's so mysterious. He's a very private person.' I wished she wouldn't keep telling me things about Beast as if I didn't know anything about him. I continued trying to harvest the croissant crumbs. 'The fact is, I can't quite make out if he's got a girlfriend or not.' She stared at me, blushing slightly and trying to make her curiosity look casual. 'Has he?'

I finished chewing my mouthful of croissant. It seemed to have taken ten years. There were still flakes of pastry stuck to my lips. I must have looked like a snake shedding its skin. I tried to steer the flakes mouthwards with my little finger. My finger, too, became caked with lipgloss and croissant crumbs. Maybe it was a blessing I hadn't seen Beast today after all.

'My impression is,' I said, giving in to a cruel impulse which nevertheless was fully justified, 'that he has a different girlfriend every day of the week.'

Charlie looked crushed for a split second – a minor victory for me. What I'd said was a throwback to the old Beast. I hadn't seen him with a girl recently, apart from her. But Charlie mustn't know that.

'Zoe, I need your advice.' She lowered her voice and leaned in confidentially. I could smell her perfume. It was delicious and spicy. Her skin was flawless and a divine coffee colour. 'The thing is,' she whispered, 'I think Beast really likes me, but he hasn't actually said anything . . . and I have to admit, I really, really, *really* like him.'

I was almost physically sick at this news, even though I'd been half-expecting it.

'Next time you see him,' she went on, 'would you mind just probing discreetly – because you've been friends for so long, you can do this without it seeming weird – just try and find out if he's seeing anybody. And try and find out what he thinks about me. You know. Discreetly. If you wouldn't mind?' She reached across the table and gave my arm a desperate, grateful squeeze.

I nodded, because it wasn't possible to speak for a moment. And I shoved another massive helping of croissant into my mouth. It was either that or smash it in her face, which was, at this early stage in our relationship at least, maybe not such a good idea. However, I didn't totally rule it out for later.

Chapter 11

After my ordeal with Charlie I had a couple of hours to kill before I was due to meet Chloe outside the town hall. Toby texted me to say he was around so we agreed to meet. I didn't want to drift round town alone. I knew I would only torment myself with thoughts of Charlie and Beast. Deeply though I hated Charlie, I could see she was one hundred per cent gorgeous and if she was mad about Beast, he would clearly fall for her as soon as he could fit it into his busy schedule.

'Hello, daaaarling!' Toby whooped, flapping his hands about. 'How about an early lunch? I'm on a 30,000-calories-a-day diet!'

'No, Tobe! Bad dog!' I growled playfully. I didn't feel hungry at all. My croissant was lying evilly in my stomach like a crocodile at the bottom of a very foul swamp.

'How about coming round my place tonight to watch some DVDs?' asked Tobe.

'Uhhh . . . well, Chloe was going to come round mine,' I pondered. 'Our parents are away. We were going to do our exercise video and stuff.'

'Oh go on, Zoe! Ferg is coming! We're getting an Indian takeaway! Put the diet on hold!'

'I can't start guzzling curries for a while, Tobe!' I wailed, slapping my hips. 'Look at my flab!'

'Rubbish!' retorted Toby. 'You'll fade away, you're so tiny! Anyway, you don't have to have the curry. You could just have the cucumber raita!'

'We've got to stop talking about food all the time,' I said sternly. 'Come on! Let's do two circuits of the park! We've got to shed our porky personas and become lithe and slinky!' I kept thinking about Charlie and her speckly eyes and trim hips and fabulous mascara and tawny skin. She smelled of citrus and jasmine. I hadn't got a hope.

'What's my worst feature?' I asked Tobe, as we entered the park and headed for the bandstand.

'Nothing, daaarrrling!' he drawled. 'You're one hundred per cent perfect!'

'Let's walk faster, Tobe!' I urged, although it was quite a struggle for me, because my jeans were so tight.

'Can't!' puffed Tobe. 'Let's sit down!'

We arrived at the adventure playground. I know people our age aren't supposed to go on the swings and stuff, but I'm always strangely tempted by the rope slide, and that's for older kids anyway, and it only has a weight restriction of 'under 120 kg'. It's comforting to know that's a category I can still squeeze into.

Toby lowered himself down on to the deck of a pirate-ship climbing frame, closed his eyes and took in some autumnal rays. I dropped my bag beside him, had a quick look to make sure nobody was about, then ran to the rope slide, grabbed the rope and launched myself down the wire with a massive leap. As the trees and grass flashed past, my tummy turned over in a very similar way to whenever I saw Beast.

'Wheeeeeeeee!' I yelled. Wow! I'll never get too old for the rope slide. Even when I'm forty-two with my high-powered job in the City, I'll still come home every weekend in order to go whizzing past the little kids.

As I jumped off at the other end and hastily pulled

down my top to cover the dodgy hip area, Toby shouted something.

'What?' I called.

'Your phone rang!'

Typical! My phone always yells if I leave it alone for a split second – a bit like a baby crying, I imagine. Presumably this was Chloe changing the time of our meeting or something. Maybe she was in town already. I rummaged for my phone in the hellish depths of my bag. Oh no! It was a voicemail from Beast!

'Uhhh, Zoe,' he said, 'sorry to miss you when you called by the office this morning. Thanks for offering to help with Jailhouse Rock, that's brilliant. I've got another meeting now – uh – I'll have to switch my phone off, but I'll ring you tonight and we can talk about it.'

Anguish at having missed Beast's call flooded through me, rapidly followed by excited anticipation of talking to him tonight.

'What's wrong, sunshine?' enquired Toby. He'd seen my face perform a thousand strange man-oeuvres. I couldn't call Beast back and leave a message, not with Toby watching and eavesdropping.

'Oh, nothing, I just missed Beast,' I said, trying for

a light, unconcerned, throwaway tone.

'Zoe?' asked Toby softly. He can be very percep-tive, for a boy. I looked up into his baby-blue eyes. 'Are you . . . and Beast . . . an item?' His eyes were dancing in a naughty teasing way.

'No, of course not!' I retorted, too hastily, blushing. 'I'm just annoyed I missed him twice today.'

Toby stared at me. He wasn't convinced. I saved Beast's message so I could secretly listen to it over and over again a hundred times, then I turned away from Toby and headed for the aviary. I wanted to hide my face in case Toby spotted more telltale signs, so I pretended to have a sudden interest in birds . . . I stared at the mynah birds and parrots, though in a funny way I didn't register what I was seeing. The thought of Beast blotted everything else out. Toby arrived at my side.

'You've got a thing about Beast!' he grinned taunt-ingly. There was a mischievous glint in his eyes which frankly terrified me because Motormouth Toby's the biggest gossip in school. I could see he was already planning to broadcast it to the world first thing on Monday morning. In fact, why wait till then? He'd probably send a group email round his contact list, which included famous gossips in five continents.

'No, I have *not* got a thing about Beast!' I tried one more time to deny it. But my hands were trembling, my cheeks were bright scarlet and I could feel my neck throbbing visibly as my poor little heart tried to cope with the stress.

'Yes, you have!' Toby's face broke into a broad, teasing smile. He looked like a cat that has just discovered a prize salmon in a deserted kitchen. 'So when did all this happen? I thought you hated him?! Amazing!'

'Toby.' Hastily I abandoned my attempt to bluff it out. 'I want you to swear on the sacred name of Princess Diana that you will never ever whisper a word of this to anybody.' Princess Diana is Toby's most sacred icon. He has huge photos of her on his wall.

'So it's true then?' grinned Toby, looking triumphant and not at all sacred.

'I'll tell you the details if you swear not to breathe a word of this to anybody,' I said. '*Particularly* Chloe. I will literally kill you seven different ways if you mention it to her. But seriously, don't mention it to anybody at all. I know you. You sing like a goddam canary.'

'OK, OK,' said Toby eagerly. 'I swear I won't utter a single peep!'

'On the sacred name . . . ?'

'On the sacred name of Princess Diana,' he said, in a special royal and sacred voice, with his hand on his heart.

'*Hello!*' came a voice from nearby. I jumped – had somebody crept up on us and heard the lot? Oh no – phew! It was only a mynah bird. The birds in the aviary seemed to be eavesdropping. But even if Toby managed to control himself, there was no guarantee that the mynah birds wouldn't confide the saucy details to anyone who passed by their cage: *Hello! Guess what! Zoe's got a thing about Beast! He's a pretty boy!*

'How did it start?' Toby asked, his whole porky little body vibrating with curiosity.

'Nothing's going on,' I replied bleakly.

'But you *lurve* him!'

'Well, I like him, anyway,' I admitted edgily. 'But it's purely a one-way street.'

'So why did he call just now?'

'To give me some orders about leaflets, I assume,' I said, shrugging. 'I went round to the office this morning to offer to help. He wasn't there so I had coffee with his gorgeous PA. So that's how I came to miss him twice.'

'Are you helping with Jailhouse Rock, then?' asked Tobe. 'Me and Ferg are going to as well. So we'll have a ringside seat if anything happens on the *lurve* front.'

'It's the PA you want to watch,' I grumbled. 'She looks like a freakin' angel.'

'Who wants an angel?' giggled Toby. 'Give me a cute little devil any day!'

'Don't tell Chloe any of this.' My spine went cold at the thought of Toby gossiping away for England. 'And *please* don't tell her I'm helping with Jailhouse Rock, either.'

'Why not?'

'Because she had a thing about Beast once and sent him nuisance love texts.'

Toby's eyes grew huge. Another salmon for Pussy! Oh God! What had I done? What a terrible, terrible thing to say! How could I have let that slip? I was a monster of indiscretion! I deserved to have my tongue cut out and made into pies, like somebody in a fairytale.

'Chloe sent Beast nuisance love texts?!' he drooled.

'No, no, I didn't mean that! I mean, it was nothing, it was over ages ago, just don't ever mention that to anybody – forget I said it!' I warned sharply.

'Chloe would be mortified and she would literally kill me. If you ever so much as hint it to her I will cut you out of my will, and you and I will be finished for ever!'

'OK, no need to go ballistic,' grinned Tobe. 'I'm the soul of discretion, you know that.'

Chapter 12

Luckily Tobe behaved very well when we met Chloe, and he went off shortly afterwards to meet Ferg, who wasn't free till lunchtime because he had a Saturday morning job. I shuddered with remorse that I had let slip the details about Chloe's nuisance love texts, and prayed fervently that Toby would resist the temptation to spill the beans. Although I love nothing more than receiving all his latest goss, I would have to emigrate to the Extremely Faraway Islands if Chloe's embarrassing secret became widely known because of me.

'Right, brilliant, now we're going to find the dresses that are going to turn us into goddesses,' said Chloe. 'Dresses for Goddesses! OK? And you've got to be really firm with me if I get fixated on something dire.'

'And you do the same for me,' I added sportingly, even though I had no intention of trying on anything less than divine.

We plunged into the first store. Chloe raced about enthusiastically, gathering armfuls of dresses to try on. She zoomed in on pink, tiered numbers, ruffled prom dresses and one very long vintage floral frock. However, I was having the opposite problem. I'd decided you couldn't go wrong with black, and of course it had to be short – Jailhouse Rock was only a concert, after all – but the black dresses all looked so dull, as if they were designed for grannies to wear at funerals.

Eventually I selected a strapless corsage dress with a kind of balloony skirt and sequins around the neck-line, a black tiered mini and a floaty ensemble that had black chiffon-like scarves hanging down the front. Although it was bizarre, I was hoping it might hide my tum and thighs – although I still had a couple of weeks to get trim and shed the flab before Jailhouse Rock.

We piled into a changing booth and ripped off our kit. Chloe dived into the pink tiered thing; I struggled into the strapless mushroom-shaped number. It was hopeless trying it on with my bra straps showing, so I wriggled out of the top of the dress, discarded my bra and tried to wriggle back in. Chloe suddenly straightened up and ran her fingers through her hair with a flamboyant gesture. Her elbow smacked into my right eye.

'Ow! Ow! God, that hurt!' I gasped, trying not to screech too loudly and jumping up and down in agony while cradling my throbbing eye socket. With the other, undamaged eye I could clearly see that I hadn't managed to get both boobs safely back inside the top of the dress, and they were flouncing about like bouncy castles in a storm.

'My God! Zoe! I'm so sorry!' cried Chloe, panicking wildly in case she had given me a fatal blow.

'It's OK! It's OK!' I assured her gallantly, though convinced that my eye socket was actually cracked. At this point a sales assistant, alerted perhaps by the noise coming from our cubicle (the sound, I have to admit, of a fox in a poultry shed), arrived at our door.

'Everything all right?' she called over the low door; not looking in, but horribly *nearly*. 'How's it going?'

'Brilliant! Brilliant!' I gasped, grabbing my boobs in alarm and trying to force them back down into the crumpled corsage.

'Everything's fine, thanks!' Chloe called, and thank God, the sales assistant went away.

'Why do they *do* that?' I whispered indignantly. 'I mean, being in here . . . it's private. Almost like being in the loo. Restroom attendants don't start knocking on the door after half a minute and say, *"How are you getting on?"*'

'Oh no! Why did you have to say that? I'm going to have a horrible dream now!' Chloe got the giggles at this point.

By now my agony had subsided into mere pain, though I was pretty sure I was going to be sporting a black eye for the next few days. I blinked blearily at my mirror image. The top of the dress was still somehow jammed under my boobs, and the sequinned edge had turned in on itself and was beginning to itch like mad against my lower ribcage. My hair was ruffled up like a hedge and my right eye was red and streaming. There was mascara all down my cheek.

'How's this for style?' I demanded, striking a bold pose whilst still essentially topless and hideous.

'Definitely goddess-like,' squealed Chloe in hysterics. 'You could paint faces on your boobs – that would be supernatural! And look at me: I look like a freakin' cake!'

112

'Quite a classy one, though,' I mused, admiring her layers of ruffled pink. 'You could dust your cleavage with icing sugar.'

'And we could dot my hair with tasteful little blobs of whipped cream!' screamed Chloe (though as silently as possible: we didn't want to be asked to leave).

We struggled out of our dresses (though Chloe had to pull me out of mine) and hastily tried on the others, even though I already had a sinking feeling about the whole project. Chloe's ruffled prom dress made her look like some kind of weird Amazonian lizard and her long vintage floral number transformed her into a chihuahua lost in a flower bed. My black tiered mini turned me into a stack of car tyres, whilst somehow revealing my legs as a pair of giant sausages, and the thing with the black chiffon scarves hanging down the front suggested an explosion in a curtain factory. We were clearly not going to score here, so we moved on.

During the next couple of hours we tried on dresses that made us look like giraffes, pizzas, air bags, chickens, wheelie bins, low-budget ghosts, and, worst of all perhaps, airline stewardesses. Then, suddenly, in the window of a funny little boutique called Razzmatazz, I saw it.

It was a pink satiny number, off the shoulder, on the money, out of this world. It was short, sizzling, slinky, shimmering, sexy, sensational. Yes, I quite liked it in a way.

'Awesome!' I shouted, grabbing Chloe's arm. We raced inside, found the rail and, thank goodness, there was still one available in my size. I dived into it in desperate panic, praying it wouldn't look too awful, like all the other dresses I'd tried on in the past couple of hours. But the result was just amazing. I stared at myself in disbelief: the image in the mirror looked like somebody else, somebody relaxed and even charming. Was this really me?

'Wow!' breathed Chloe. 'Now you really *do* look like a goddess!' Somehow, I don't know how, the dress was the perfect thing for me. I had always dreamed of looking like this, but never believed it was possible. 'You've gotta have it!' urged Chloe. 'How much?'

It wasn't cheap, but it wasn't totally out of reach. I begged the sales assistant to let me put a deposit on it and come back next week with the rest. She was a kind motherly sort of woman, and she agreed. While she was writing out the details for her records, Chloe sighed.

'I'm so happy for you, Zoe,' she said. 'But I wish I'd managed to find something.'

'You will, babe,' I assured her. The sales lady looked up, and smiled at Chloe.

'You're so tiny!' she said. 'So lucky! Have you tried the little black number with the sequinned neckline?'

Chloe looked doubtful. 'Black?' she said.

'No harm in trying it on,' said the woman. 'They're over there. You can't go wrong with black. Perfect for redheads.'

Chloe tried it on. It was a really cute mini, in a kind of stretchy material, with a high empire waist and a sparkling neckline. It looked sensational.

'Black?' frowned Chloe dubiously, looking at me with an uncertain frown.

'Chloe, you look the business!' I assured her. 'It's scrumptious! So elegant!' I was tempted to say that she didn't have to be festooned with tortoises to look good, but I thought it would be more tactful to hold back.

'I do sort of like it . . .' Chloe hesitated.

'Of course you do!' I insisted. 'It's your goddess frock! So we've found them both! Sorted!'

Although paying for them was going to be a struggle. Neither of us could afford to pay up on the spot and the sales assistant said she could only keep them for a few days. We were going to have to get our hands on some cash – and fast.

Chapter 13

'Right,' said Chloe, as we settled down by the PC with our cups of zingy ginger and lemon herbal tea. We'd had our baked-jacket spuds, and I'd made a special salad with olives and anchovies. We were now ready to rock. 'Do a search on *goddesses*.' I Googled it up.

'There's a quiz! A goddess quiz!' yelled Chloe. Two clicks and we were there. '"*Discover your goddess type!*"'

'"*Grow your inner goddess!*"' I yelled, clicking like a mad click-beetle.

'"*Your road to growth and inspiration!*"' shrieked Chloe. We soon discovered, though, that it cost $19.75 to take the Goddess Quiz.

'What a rip-off!' I grumbled. 'I'm sure the

goddesses would be outraged.'

'The goddess of money might be quite impressed,' pondered Chloe.

'Who needs a stupid quiz, anyway? We can find out everything we need to know by ourselves. A real goddess wouldn't take a quiz to find out what sort of goddess she was.'

'Indian goddesses are cool!' suggested Chloe. 'Let's have a look at them!'

Soon we were admiring a picture of Kali, sometimes known as the nude Indian goddess of evil.

'Well, that's *so* me, obviously,' I sighed in rapture. 'Look: "*For earrings she wears two dead bodies and she has a necklace of skulls.*" That is so the look I was planning for this winter.'

'The dead bodies as earrings idea is attractive, obviously,' said Chloe. 'But wouldn't they drag your earlobes down a bit?'

'Not if they were dead mice or spiders,' I mused. 'Oh no, wait – I'd need a garland of fifty human heads, apparently. I'm not sure I could get away with that in school. Maybe Kali is a bit too challenging as a role model.'

'Look, though,' said Chloe, peering at the screen. 'Her sword "*cuts the knots of ignorance and destroys false consciousness*". Cool!'

'False consciousness is a problem, though,' I added. 'I mean, how do you know if your consciousness is false or not?'

'Find another goddess,' urged Chloe. Within moments we were devouring the details of the Norse goddess Freya. It said she was often depicted travelling in a chariot pulled by two blue cats.

'Blue cats!' exclaimed Chloe. 'Great fashion statement! I like Freya. Show me more!'

'Her husband Od was lost at sea but when she was reunited with him he had been turned into a sea monster.'

'Typical man!' snorted Chloe. 'So unreliable. I wouldn't mind a husband called Od, though. *"Can I introduce my husband, Od?"* It would be kind of a talking point.'

'Very Od,' I agreed. 'She remained devoted to him even though he was a sea monster,' I read on. 'Oh dear . . . but he was killed, in the end. Bad luck!'

'Tough!' sighed Chloe. 'I was kind of getting into Od, even with all his tentacles and slime.'

'Couldn't be worse than Joe Gibbons in the lower sixth,' I observed. 'Oh look! It's all right, after all, because the rest of the gods allowed him to have conjugal visits.'

'What are conjugal visits?' asked Chloe. We weren't quite sure so we looked it up on Wikipedia. Apparently a conjugal visit is where a prison inmate can be visited in private by his wife in a little cell with a bed and stuff, so they can get up to all sorts of hanky-panky.

'Gross!' shrieked Chloe. 'I was really into Freya because of the blue cats, but now I know she sleeps with a sea monster who is also a ghost, I've gone off her big time!'

'So have I. Let's go to Venus. These minor goddesses are letting us down.'

There were some great paintings of Venus, but we decided she wasn't a good role model either because, basically, she seemed to be obsessed with men. Well, she was the goddess of love, so she had a good excuse. But still . . .

'Look up some British goddesses,' suggested Chloe. 'Think Local!'

At this point my mobile rang. Instantly my heart leapt right out of my mouth and performed two circuits of the room: it had to be Beast. I grabbed my moby and ran out into the hall.

'Yes???!!' I hissed in frantic excitement, though trying, of course, to sound laid-back, cool and divine.

'Hello, old boy, this is your lovable old pa,' said Dad. 'How's it going?'

'Fine, Dad!' I trilled, trying to conceal my disappointment with an anguished screech of delight. 'Chloe and I are doing some research on goddesses!' I hoped he would be impressed by our scholarly programme. 'What are you up to?'

'Having a lovely supper in a little pub called the Vine Tree,' said Dad. 'So you're OK, then?'

'So far . . . but we've left the front door wide open with a notice saying: "*Werewolves, please walk right in.*" '

'Well, let's hope they do,' said Dad. 'But really, you should have booked ahead. Werewolves are always so busy on Saturday night.'

'I know.'

'Mum says how did the shopping trip go?'

'Brilliant! I found this amazing dress! But, Dad! Listen! If I clean the house from top to bottom will you pay me?' There was a sudden nasty little silence.

'Let's talk about that when we get back,' he said.

'No! Discuss it now! How much per room!?'

'Oh, I don't know. Which rooms were you thinking of cleaning?'

'All of them! Any of them!'

'Well, don't go into my study, that's all. The crumbs on the carpet are supposed to be there – and I know the exact location of every one!'

'No probs, Dad! OK. Bye!' I didn't want to clog up the line with endless Dad-talk when Beast might ring at any moment.

'Bye already?' Dad sounded startled.

'Yeah! Must keep phone bill down!' I had started to talk in some weird code, using fewer words, either to keep bill down or ditch Dad *now*.

'OK, OK! Bye then, old boy!'

'Love you! See you tomorrow!' I went back to the sitting room. 'That was my dad,' I told Chloe unnecessarily. 'He said they'll pay me to clean the house!' Though this wasn't strictly what Dad had actually said, I had high hopes. And I'd suddenly realised that, if I got Chloe busy with housework, preferably vacuuming on the top floor, she wouldn't be able to overhear any phone call I might have with Beast.

'Great!' she smiled, looking somehow innocent and vulnerable because I was planning to enslave her domestically. I felt horrid, but it had to be done. Anyway, when Beast used to call *her*, months ago, she'd always run off to another room so I couldn't overhear.

'I've found another goddess!' said Chloe, looking up from the PC screen. 'She's called Axo Mama and she's the goddess of potatoes.'

'Look, I know how important spuds are to you, Chloe,' I smiled treacherously, 'but let's give the Internet a rest for a bit, shall we? We have to clean the house.' Chloe looked surprised.

'What, now?' she asked.

'Yeah, why not?' I countered, going off towards the kitchen. 'Come on! No time like the present! It'll be great exercise and we can share the muns.'

'But I think my dad will pay for my dress!' complained Chloe, following me reluctantly towards the sink. I opened the cupboard doors below, where all the cleaning stuff is kept.

'Well, that's great for you,' I said. 'Terrific! But I've got to work for mine. Of course you don't have to help me, but I'm going to do a couple of hours of housework right now, and if you do help me I'll owe you, big time. And if you don't help me I shall turn into the goddess Kali and cut your head off just slightly, because refusing to help me would be a sign of false consciousness, OK?'

Chapter 14

'OK,' sighed Chloe in a martyred way. Still, at least she was on board. 'What do you want me to do?' I pretended to think for a moment.

'Vacuuming?' I suggested, walking through to the cupboard under the stairs. 'It's terrific exercise and I read somewhere it develops the bust, which is why I'd rather not do it myself as my boobs are getting a bit unmanageable. I turned over in bed last night and one socked me on the jaw and almost knocked me out.' Chloe giggled.

At this very moment – only two minutes too early, my moby rang again. And this time the magic word HARRY flashed up – Beast's real name, and the one he'd used when he entered his number into my phone, back in Newquay. Yes, his divine hands had once touched this phone . . . And now his divine voice was going to enter my car with Chloe right next to me, standing there eavesdropping.

'Oh, hi!' I tried to sound casual, as if I'd forgotten he existed, but was slightly pleased to have been reminded.

'Hi!' said Beast. 'Uh, Zoe. Sorry I missed you this morning.'

'Oh, errr, it doesn't matter.' If Chloe hadn't been eavesdropping, I could have said that I was really sorry to have missed him, too. But I had to keep my replies short and non-committal. I was already planning to try and disguise this, for Chloe's benefit, as another call from Dad – I was going to say he'd forgotten something and had rung back. The trouble was, this meant I couldn't say much except for the odd non-committal grunt, and from Beast's point of view, it might make me sound like a moody cow.

'Yeah, Zoe . . . I just wanted to say I'd really like your help with the poster competition. We're trying to draw up a shortlist. Could you do that for me?'

'Sure! What does it involve?'

'Oh, just looking through about a hundred kids' paintings, choosing the best five and then bringing them to a meeting at the office on Wednesday. It's an evening meeting – seven-thirty. Could you make that?'

'Yes, I think so,' I said airily, as if my diary, though full, would admit one more tiny appointment. Whereas really my diary was a howling vacuum of nothingness and I would walk barefoot through fire for half an hour with Beast, even if other people were going to be there.

'Great, thanks,' said Beast briskly. There was a little silence, as though he was wondering what to say next.

'So how are things? OK?' he asked. 'Has Tam gone back to uni?' Oh no! He wanted to talk. And I, more than anything, wanted to *talk* to him. But how could I, with Chloe following every word? As I was pretending he was my dad, who already knew Tam had gone back, I couldn't provide any details.

'Oh, yeah, a few days ago.' There was another tingling little pause.

'Zoe . . . are you OK?'

'Yes, fine!' I assured him in a rush. I suddenly knew that Beast had realised there was somebody with me, and of course he might think it was that wretched fictional boyfriend Dan, who was still hanging round in the atmosphere ruining my reputation for availability.

I had to tell Beast there was no Dan. But I couldn't mention it now. I couldn't mention anything – and being so tongue-tied, I was certain to be giving out all the wrong signals. 'I'm just about to clean out the fridge!' I added randomly, in a vain attempt to make it sound as if I was talking to my dad.

'Oh, right,' said Beast, sounding a bit mystified. 'Good idea. I must do that one day. Anyway . . . I'll bring the paintings round first thing in the morning, OK?'

'Fine,' I drawled, trying to sound cool, though I was stunned at the news that Beast would be on my doorstep at dawn, or shortly thereafter.

'See you then,' he added. 'Bye!'

'Bye!'

'Who was that?' hissed Chloe right away.

'Oh, only my dad again,' I sighed, as if I'd just had the most tiresome and boring conversation in the world, even though it had made my heart pound and my blood boil.

'Really?' Chloe peered into my face. 'Are you sure?'

'Of course I'm sure it was my dad!' I snapped, guilty and edgy. I hate lying to Chloe.

'You just sounded a bit weird.'

'He was being weird about paying me and stuff.'

'What was that about when you said, "Oh, yeah, a few days ago"?' Chloe was irritating me big time now, even though I was the one in the wrong.

'Oh, that was just about had I done my homework, etc., that history essay . . . you know. Mum didn't want me cleaning the house if I hadn't got round to doing homework yet.' I sighed, as if annoyed by parents whereas really I was fighting off an urge to hit my dearest friend. 'Anyway! Bor-ing! Let's get this show on the road! *How Clean Is Your House?* I'll be Kim, you be Aggie! If only I had a pair of rubber gloves with feathers on!'

I handed over the vacuum cleaner and asked Chloe if she'd mind vacuuming.

'Oh no!' she grinned joyfully. 'Not if it develops my bust! I'll do the whole house!' She decided to start at the top, leaving me to clean the kitchen whilst I tried to calm down after that excruciating call from Beast. But instead of calming down I became more and more agitated.

Oh my God! Beast was going to drop round tomorrow first thing! But what was first thing on a Sunday morning, exactly? In my world, it's a quarter to twelve, but Beast is a sporty type who plays rugby

128

and probably goes jogging at dawn.

It was chillingly clear to me what I had to do. First, I had to be ready at 7.15 a.m. looking effortlessly glam and goddess-like. But where was I going to find fifty human heads for my necklace? And how was I going to make sure Chloe wasn't awake and eavesdropping – or even worse, gawping – at my sacred visit from the love of my life? And of course, as Beast used to be Chloe's heart-throb, I obviously had to keep it totally secret from her for her own sake as well as mine.

My mind was whirling so wildly my head felt hot, so I opened the fridge to enjoy a cooling blast of air and was enveloped in a zoo-like stink that made my eyes water. My dad has a weakness for smelly French cheeses, and he has a horrible habit of just chucking them in the fridge without putting them back in the plastic cheese-box.

There was a horrible culprit oozing evil grey scum, so I grabbed it, wrapped it in plastic and shut it firmly in the cheese-box. But its stink seemed to have infected everything else. Although maybe that was a different disgusting smell? Bending down, I warily ransacked the salad drawer and found a plastic bag of salad leaves that had formed a slimy purée all by themselves.

'Yeaugh!' I yelled, reaching for the rubber gloves. There was also a rotten half-cabbage down there and a cucumber that had gone grey and mouldy and had liquified inside its horrid plastic sheath. The smell of all this rotting veg was diabolical. I fetched the compost bucket and slopped it all in, gagging and cursing my parents for not being able to keep a clean fridge and for exposing their darling daughter to untold health risks. All the time my mind was racing.

As I scrubbed out the fridge with detergent, I tried to draw up a plan. I could not, *absolutely* could not bear it if Chloe was up and about when Beast came round tomorrow morning. So basically I had to tire her out so completely and utterly that she would go to bed very, very late and totally exhausted.

But while it was important to tire Chloe out, if I was shattered next morning when Beast came round, it would be a disaster. I had to be gorgeous and full of energy and dazzling and irresistible – for the first and probably the only time in my life.

Chapter 15

Half an hour later Chloe arrived in the kitchen, beaming. I was scrubbing the wall behind the cooker, which was coated with grease. Once I'd cleaned the fridge out (in itself a heroic task, equal to anything the army had had to do in wartime), I'd discovered the oven was even more revolting, and that in turn had led to this wall . . .

My goddam parents! What irresponsible old hippies! This kitchen was a pit of filth! Mum always looked so swish with her Jimmy Choo shoes and her smart suits, but if her clients could take a peek inside her fridge they'd have a fit.

'I enjoyed that,' said Chloe, looking perky. 'I've put the vacuum cleaner away. What next? It's weird, I'm really getting into this housework thing.'

'How about scrubbing the kitchen floor?' I suggested recklessly. Somehow I had to wear Chloe out. Right now she looked fresher than ever.

'Brilliant! Great idea!' Chloe grabbed a broom and swept the floor, then she found the dustpan and brush and scooped up the debris, then she got out the mop and bucket. Meanwhile, I was struggling with what seemed to be a moth omelette glued to the wall behind the cooker. My arm ached with scrubbing – possibly because the only scrubbing I'd ever done before in my life had been with a make-up remover pad.

'God!' I gasped. 'I think I've strained my shoulder!' Chloe started mopping away, singing as she worked. She didn't look even remotely tired yet, whereas I was seriously flagging.

'We could start a house-cleaning business at weekends!' trilled Chloe, pirouetting around her mop and flicking water in all directions.

'Calm down!' I grumbled. 'This is a chore, not some kind of cabaret performance!'

'We could start a cabaret act based on housework!' yelled Chloe. I began to wonder if my special olive and anchovy salad was affecting her. They say fish is good for your brain and I somehow associate olives with wisdom (it's nothing to do with Popeye's wife Olive, either). Maybe her brain had gone into some demented anchovy-inspired overdrive. 'We could choreograph a whole series of moves based on vacuuming and mopping and stuff!' Chloe went on, waltzing across the kitchen on a waft of lavender'n'herb-scented eco floor-cleaner.

'Why don't we do the hip-hop workout when we've finished this?' I suggested, even though just the thought of it made me want to lie down.

'Excellent idea!' trilled Chloe. 'I'm nice and warmed up now from the vacuuming and mopping!' Chloe may have been warmed up, but I was washed up and burnt out.

'OK,' I said wearily, scraping the last of the gunge off the hotplates. 'Let's get the DVD and do it.'

First I had to change into clean clothes: my current outfit was smeared with filth and grease. I put on a loose T-shirt, shorts and trainers. We pushed back the furniture and let rip until our hips were hopped, our bellies blasted and our groins gasping for mercy.

'Phew!' I gasped, sinking down on to the sofa. 'I'm never ever going to be able to move again! My legs have turned to spaghetti!' Chloe flopped down beside me.

'Mine have turned to custard!' she panted. 'Great, though, wasn't it?'

'Brilliant,' I said. 'Hey! We should have taken videos of ourselves doing it! That would be such a laugh! We should do that now before we start to seize up!' I grabbed my digital camera.

'Come on, girl – show me your moves!' I insisted, switching the DVD back on. This was an attempt to get Chloe to do more hip hop while I restfully videoed her from the sofa.

'Aw, no!' groaned Chloe. 'I am like totally shattered! I'm gonna have a nap!' And she rested her head on a cushion and closed her eyes.

'You so are not!' I shrieked, panicking. Chloe mustn't go to sleep now! I had to keep her awake for hours and hours so she'd sleep late tomorrow morning, leaving me glamorously alone when Beast called. 'Chloe!' I knelt by the sofa and prised her eyelids open. 'Don't leave me like this! Let's do something! I feel so pumped up! Let's go for a run!'

Chloe sat up, looking puzzled. 'A run? But we've only just done the hip-hop routine. And before that we did all that housework.'

'But we've got to get fit!' I insisted. 'To become goddesses! I feel so much better already! We could

134

just jog round the block!'

'You said you didn't want to go jogging,' objected Chloe. 'After we ran round the school field you said Never Again. And it's dark now.'

'Precisely!' I cried, like a conjuror producing a rabbit from a hat. 'So nobody will be able to see our flab flapping! Come on – just once round the block!' I pulled Chloe off the sofa and towards the front door.

'Oh, all right, then,' she agreed. 'Just once round the block, though.' I grabbed the front door key and we plunged out into the night. Chloe shot off like a rocket – she can be such a show-off – and I puffed gamely along behind her. It was one of those gloomy, dripping November nights when each street lamp creates little doomed pools of lurid light. I saw Chloe race through these, one after another, like a twinkly little fairy, and disappear round the corner.

And then I heard it – behind me. A sinister padding and panting. Oh my God! Maybe there were werewolves around, after all! I whirled round, and through the murk I was terrified to see a big dog loping towards me. There was no sign of an owner (people are so irresponsible) and the dog looked mean, as if it knew I wasn't what you'd call canine-friendly. I do know one thing, though: if a strange dog comes up to you, the very worst thing you can do is turn your back and run.

Of course, that's exactly what I did. I ran like hell – and behind me I could hear the dog barking joyfully as it bounded after me, its teeth bared and its eyes fixed on my mountainous bum. And then the worst possible thing happened. I tripped. A bit of uneven pavement did for me. I literally left Planet Earth for a few seconds and went hurtling forward through the air like a small but plucky jumbo jet. I didn't take off, though, as a goddess would have done, soaring up into the clouds and leaving the dog panting admiringly in her wake. Instead I cringed in horror as the pavement loomed up and I executed a ghastly crash landing, copping the full force of the fall on the palms of my hands, my knees and, most disastrously of all, my chin.

And then, to add insult to injury, the goddam dog jumped on top of me and stuck its nose in my neck.

'Boris!' I heard a distant voice cry. 'Boris! Come here! Bad dog!'

If life were a movie, of course, the dog owner would turn out to be a handsome stranger who would chivalrously help me to my feet, escort me home, bathe my wounds and stare, enchanted, into my eyes.

Instead the dog owner was a bad-tempered middle-aged woman who said abruptly, 'Are you all right?' as I crawled to my feet.

'Absolutely! Totally!' I nodded, getting up hastily and backing off. Boris still seemed intent on either marrying me or devouring me – I wasn't quite sure – and I was relieved when I saw his owner grab his collar and attach his lead again.

I hobbled off. Running was impossible. Although I'd told Boris's owner I was *absolutely* all right, I was, in fact, completely destroyed. I could feel blood trickling down from my grazed knees, my palms were stinging like mad, and when I touched my chin there was blood all over my fingers. I decided to abandon the plan to do a circuit right round the block, and I limped back home the way I'd come, snivelling to myself in desperation. It seemed everything was against me.

Chloe arrived home around the same time, bounding up from the other direction having completed her circuit of the block. She was looking bright-eyed and fighting fit, but her face fell when she saw me.

'Oh, Zoe, babe!' she cried in horror. 'Whatever

happened?' We went in and Chloe took really good care of me: she bathed my knees and my palms and my chin with antiseptic and we found some plasters in the First Aid box. 'Poor Zoe!' she cooed. Chloe can be so nice when people are hurt. I think she should be a nurse when she leaves school. 'At least it's Sunday tomorrow! You can take things easy.'

If only she knew. As I surveyed myself in my full-length mirror I saw a casualty from a natural disaster. The bandaged knees meant a miniskirt wasn't an option; the bandaged hands were hardly going to bewitch Beast even if I applied some ravishing pearly-pink nail varnish, but my face was the worst catastrophe. Not only had I acquired a red beard of bloody scabs, but I was clearly developing a black eye from where Chloe had elbowed me in the changing booth that morning.

Normally it would have seemed an impossible job to make myself look like a goddess, just starting out in my natural state. Now I had a mountain to climb just to transform myself into a human being.

Chapter 16

I abandoned my plan to tire Chloe out. I had been punished for my horridness. But weirdly, Chloe seemed determined to tire herself out. She insisted we watch a really scary movie in which a shapeless breathing psycho stalked young girls who were all Home Alone, by hiding in their gardens, breathing murderously outside their windows . . .

'God, Chloe!' I groaned at the end. 'That was terrifying! I'm going to have to make sure all the doors and windows are double-locked!'

'Don't leave me alone!' shuddered Chloe, fastening herself to my arm. We crept around checking the locks. The kitchen was full of hideous menace. The back door, though locked and bolted top and bottom, seemed suddenly fragile.

'God, look at that door!' I whispered in panic. 'It's, like, made of cardboard! Somebody could break in with just a teaspoon, never mind an axe!'

'And then he could creep upstairs and kill us with the teaspoon!' shrilled Chloe, joining in the hysteria.

'Oh my God!' I moaned. 'We're going to have to watch some comedy before we go to bed!'

'I can't!' whimpered Chloe. 'I'm too tired!'

'You've got to!' I insisted. 'It was your idea to watch that movie!'

I found a *Simpsons* DVD and we watched two episodes, huddled up on the sofa under a blanket. It was hilarious, but when we finally switched it off, the silence was still deadly and sinister.

'I can hear horrid breathing!' I yelled in panic.

'It's me!' screamed Chloe. 'Quick! Quick! Let's go upstairs!'

We raced up to my bedroom, and locked ourselves in. I had planned for Chloe to sleep in Tam's room so when I got up early and started to prepare for Beast's visit, I wouldn't wake her up. But clearly Chloe was never going to agree to sleeping in a separate room. I have an inflatable mattress that I use whenever she stays, so we got it out and found the sleeping bag, and after some incredibly heroic dashes to the sinister bathroom, we settled down to sleep.

Chloe fell asleep immediately, lying on her back with her mouth open. I hate it when she does this, because she makes horrid noises: kind of rattlings and gaspings and snorts and mutters. She was lying on the mattress on the floor right next to my bed, so every sound was almost in my face. Also I was going to have problems getting out of bed without treading on her.

I had to get to sleep right now. I was shattered, but it was hard to switch off because so many parts of my bod were still stinging from my fall, plus my mind was racing with thoughts of Beast. I set my moby to wake me with a discreet vibrate at six-thirty and put it under my pillow. Luckily I'm a very light sleeper. Now I absolutely had to wind down.

The house was silent, but suddenly I noticed the sound of footsteps – creak, creak, creak! Oh my God! My blood froze, my heart lurched and my knees went weak, even though I was lying down. There was somebody coming up the stairs: creak, creak, creak! Creak, creak, creak, creak, creak, creak, creak, creak . . . wait a minute! How many freakin' stairs did we have in this house?

I realised that the sound of the stealthy footsteps

was, in fact, my own blood circulating in my own ears. I had to stop panicking like this. I had to get some beauty sleep because Beast would be on my doorstep First Thing.

What was I going to wear? Mentally I did an inventory of my wardrobe: it was all garbage. But it had to be perfect – and it had to be Sunday morning-ish. I mustn't look as if I'd been tarting myself up for hours, even though that was precisely what I was going to have to do.

The best thing would be weekend casual: a white T-shirt and a denim skirt. But I knew the best T-shirt was dirty and the denim skirt was probably lying in the corner, crumpled up, under a heap of video games and other junk. I pulled the covers over my head, squeezed my eyes shut and tried in vain to empty my brain.

Twenty minutes passed, and I was still wide awake. Should I wear my black jeans or my blue dress? What did I really look like *from behind* in my black jeans? If only Chloe wasn't here, I could have got out of bed, put the light on and tried on a dozen outfits.

Twenty more minutes passed, and suddenly it was morning and there was a knock on the door, and I flew downstairs and opened the door, and there stood

Beast, only somehow he looked a bit like the guy who works in the post office, and suddenly I realised I was in my bra and pants – oh horror! I twitched awake. It was only a dream.

Chloe stirred in her sleep and said, 'Oh, I don't think so' in a totally ordinary, rather grown-up voice. What an idiot! She thought she was being so darned mature in that fantasy world of hers, and in reality she was lying on my floor clutching my cuddly duck.

It made me panic that Chloe was sleeping so soundly, whereas I was restless and jittery. Maybe she would wake early and refreshed, ready to entertain Beast, while I would fall into a concrete slumber and remain stapled to my pillow until noon.

I tried seventeen times to fall asleep, had about a hundred tiny catnaps and some really terrible dreams, in the last of which I was being eaten alive by a man from Bolton who had bad eyesight and thought I was an oyster.

Suddenly it was morning. I looked at my phone. Six-thirty. I'd had enough of trying to sleep. Even though I felt hollow and sick with fatigue, I must get up and make myself irresistible. It would be awful if I slept through the alarm and when Beast rang the doorbell, nobody answered.

Getting out of bed was a major challenge. To avoid treading on Chloe, I had to crawl to the foot of the bed and climb gingerly over the footboard. Halfway over, my groins twanged in a horrible warning: I was stiff as a board from the hip hop, the scrubbing, the jogging and, of course, the fall. Once both my feet were safely and securely on the floor (I realised now how often I'd underestimated that little treat), I made my way to the wardrobe. And when I say made my way, well, it couldn't really be described as walking. In order to minimise the pain of my stiff muscles, I had to creep along with my legs wide apart, like a cross between a crab and a coffee table.

Carefully I opened the wardrobe door. 'EEEEEEEEEEEUW!' it squealed. The bitch! I would give it a good kicking later, when Chloe had gone. Right now it had stirred her from her deepest sleep. She turned over, muttering to herself.

'I've never really liked her . . .' she sighed, then dropped back into unconscious bliss. I hoped she wasn't talking about me. Who was she talking to, in her precious dream? I wasn't just jealous of Chloe for being able to sleep: I was jealous of the people she might be meeting in her dreams, behind my back. God! If I was this possessive with my best mate, whatever would I be like if I ever got a boyfriend?

Luckily, I didn't have to make jangly noises with hangers in my wardrobe because I'd gone through an untidy phase recently, so all my clothes were in a great heap in there. I scooped out an armful at random and carried them towards the door, still walking with my legs apart with every muscle screaming in protest.

Now I had to unlock the door without waking Chloe. I dumped the heap of clothes and turned the key as quietly as possible: in other words, it only went 'SNICKETY-SNACK!' with sudden, violent, brain-shredding loudness. Chloe didn't move. I turned the doorhandle: 'CROCKLEWHINGE BARRATRAPPLE!' I opened the door, slowly, cautiously: 'SCREEEEEEENGING WHEEEEEE-EEENINGER!'

'Please, God,' I whispered, 'make Chloe sleep on. If you do, I promise I'll never be a bad girl again.'

But actually I was a bad girl again right away. A really sneaky thought suddenly occurred to me: if I locked the door behind me, Chloe wouldn't be able to gatecrash my tender early morning love-fest with Beast even if she did wake up. I could tell Chloe that I'd had to go into Tam's room because of her snoring, and I'd locked her in so she'd be safe from the horrible breathing stalker-thing with his murderous teaspoon.

Stealthily I removed the key from the lock, and after shifting my clothes mountain into Tam's room, I closed my bedroom door and locked it from the outside. Then I paused and listened. Chloe hadn't stirred. It was horrid of me, but it wasn't really cruel, because all she had to do was yell and of course I'd leave what I was doing and unlock the door *immediately*. Even if Beast was being particularly loving.

'I've always adored you, Zoe – you're a legend! I just love your beard of scabs and black eye: everyone in Hollywood will want one,' he would say.

'Heeeeeeelp!' That would be Chloe from upstairs. *'Let me out!'*

''Scuse me,' I'd say enchantingly, *'must just see to my slave.'* I'd go upstairs, unlock the door, and tell her to stay where she was and to go back to bed, because a man had come to measure up the kitchen or something.

I set up base camp in Tam's bedroom, tried on four dozen different outfits, and eventually chose skinny black jeans and an empire-line top. I tried thirteen different lipsticks, and finally settled for a mixture of

Wild Rose and Carnival. I tried five thousand different earrings, before deciding to wear no earrings at all. They would only draw attention to my weird small ears.

To pass the time until First Thing, I sat awkwardly on the sofa reading *Heat* magazine, like a guest in my own home or somebody waiting to see the dentist. There wasn't a sound from upstairs. I hoped Chloe would snore on till noon. There was no danger of her being woken by the front doorbell, as it's a bit feeble and tinny and you can't really hear it from my bedroom.

Eventually, at about nine-thirty, the doorbell gave a feeble tweet. Catapulted from the sofa by a rocket of pure love, I raced to the front door and flung it open, trying to hide the adoration and excitement that were flooding through every fibre of my being, and also hoping my scabby beard, black eye and strange table-like stance would not be too obvious.

But my love god was not there. Instead I had to feast my famished eyes on the khaki stare and limp slicked-back hair of King Nerd. 'Oh.' My heart sank like a stone. 'Matthew.'

'Paolo,' he corrected me. 'Remember? Beast asked me to drop these round.' He was carrying a big packet which I assumed must be the children's paintings. 'Something came up and he couldn't make it. Can I come in for a minute? I need to show you what to do. Explain it.'

Chapter 17

'Yeah, of course, come in.' I stood aside and Matthew draped himself over the threshold. As he passed, I got a whiff of his aftershave – although Matthew was light years away from being able to produce stubble, so I suppose in his case it should have been called before-shave. It wasn't unpleasant, but there was far too much of it for so early on a Sunday morning: it was like being visited by a Ukrainian lemonade factory. 'Go through to the kitchen,' I suggested. 'Would you like a coffee?'

Oh *why* had I said that? Was I stark staring bonkers? It was the casual throwaway little phrase I had been rehearsing all night, to lure Beast into my love den. My stupid tired brain! I had just blurted it out to the last boy on Earth I wanted to have coffee with: the boy I wanted to leave immediately, ideally before he'd even arrived.

'Oh thanks, yeah, I'd love that,' said Matthew, stopping suddenly in the kitchen and turning to look at me. I received the full blast of his breath in my face, and it wasn't pleasant. It reminded me slightly of sick. If Matthew and I were the last people left on Earth, I'm afraid the human race would have to die out. Matthew stared at me rather rudely as I filled the kettle.

'What's happened?' he asked. 'Have you been in a fight?'

'What? Oh, the black eye? Yeah, ha ha! A fight with Chloe. Not really. She elbowed me by accident.'

'And the . . .' Matthew indicated the chin area on his own face, drawing attention to a constellation of spots which reminded me of my own dear Nigel, whom I had taken pains to hide beneath a thick layer of plastered-on concealer.

'Yeah, I fell down yesterday while I was out jogging,' I admitted. 'My hands are street pizzas.' I displayed them. 'And my knees.' Matthew looked attentively at my knees, safely encased in their black skinny jeans. Thank God I had not injured my boobs – that would have given him carte blanche.

'God!' he said. 'They look terrible!' I was annoyed for a split second that he had dared to use the word 'terrible' in relation to my appearance. He should have put it differently, especially as he was in my kitchen waiting for a cup of my coffee, liberally laced with my milk and, being Matthew, about five of my sugars. He should have said, *'Never mind, you're still magnificent.'* No, wait! That was what Beast should have said, if he hadn't been too goddam lazy to turn up.

I was now getting over the shock of seeing Matthew rather than Beast, and becoming quite angry with them both.

'Decaff?' I hissed aggressively. 'Or not?'

'It depends how it was decaffeinated,' murmured Matthew, staring accusingly at my coffee jar. 'If it was decaffeinated with carbon dioxide, that's fine, but some companies use chemicals.' I seized the jar and read the label, trying hard to hide my rage. Now he was dissing my coffee!

'It says it was decaffeinated by a natural process,' I informed him crisply. 'I'm having some anyway.'

'Well, it depends what they mean by "natural",' said Matthew with an irritated sigh.

'Matthew!' I snapped. 'Do you want decaff or not?'

'Paolo,' he said. 'Yes, OK.' I noticed that he didn't say 'please' or 'thank you'. I was turning into a headmistress again, of the old-fashioned, ferocious sort.

'Seven sugars as usual?' I enquired archly.

'No, no!' said Matthew loftily. 'I've given up sugar. I never took seven anyway. That would be ridiculous.'

'It was supposed to be a joke,' I informed him sarcastically. 'Anyway . . .' I placed his coffee on the table, and to my alarm, he took this as an invitation to sit down. He sat down heavily and with a sort of finality as if he was planning to be in our kitchen for several decades.

I sat down opposite him. I would have stayed standing, to hint by body language that he shouldn't stay long, but I was so damn tired I was longing to just lie down, and sitting was the next best thing.

'So, what's to explain?' I enquired.

Matthew opened up the package and pulled out a huge pile of children's paintings.

'We want you to look at these paintings and decide which is the best,' he explained in his tortoise-like, obvious, plonking way. I hated the way he'd expressed it: '*we*' want '*you*' to do this. As if he and Beast were part of a blessed company of superior beings up on some divine pink mountaintop, peering down through the clouds and conjuring up little tasks for us Neanderthals toiling below.

'OK, fine,' I said briskly, and in my attempt to get Matthew out of the door ASAP, I sipped my coffee much too early, and scalded my tongue.

'The way we're going to do it,' he went on, moving a few of the paintings around and staring at them, 'is to draw up a sort of shortlist. We want you to chose the best five –'

'Well, yeth, obviouthly,' I interrupted, annoyed that my scalded tongue was temporarily affecting my ability to pronounce the letter 'S', because in normal circumstances I would have liked to hiss at him like a furious little puff adder. If indeed puff adders hiss. My knowledge of zoology is not even basic, I admit. 'Beatht told me that. Looking at children'th painting, it'th not rocket thienthe.'

'I know, I know . . . I'm being a bit stupid, really, but for a reason,' said Matthew, pushing the paintings aside. Then he raised his strange khaki eyes to mine and gave me a long tortured look. Oh my God! Matthew was going to hit on me! A dreadful sickening feeling spread through my tummy. If only I hadn't tired out Chloe last night! If only she was sitting right here beside me now, he'd never dare to look at me like that.

'I want your advice, really,' said Matthew, looking bashful and brushing imaginary crumbs off our kitchen table.

'Yeah, what?' I tried to look and sound as ugly as possible: I dropped my lower lip in a kind of sub-human sneer, and pushed my hair back to reveal my horrid little ears. He couldn't hit on a girl with ears that looked like squashed figs, surely.

'There's this girl . . .' Matthew stared helplessly at me. His eyes went all glistening, like boiled sweets. Another wave of nausea swept over me. I tried hard to look like a bulldog. I so desperately wanted to smell bad, too, but I had made myself so fragrant for Beast that it was an impossible task, and there's never a fart around when you want one. 'She doesn't know I like her, yet . . .' he went on. 'What I really want to know is, should I say anything?'

'But Matthew! What about Tinkerbell?'

'Trixiebell,' Matthew corrected me, looking offended. I still couldn't tell if she really was a real girlfriend, or some kind of carefully cultivated fantasy. 'I had to finish with her,' he said firmly but with a tasteful note of regret. 'She was cramping my style.'

'But she was so talented!'

'In every relationship there's a leader and a follower,' Matthew informed me in a preachy voice. 'I have to lead, because Jupiter was in my sixth house when I was born. In Swindon.'

'Well, of course you have to lead, Matthew! That's obvious.'

'Paolo,' he corrected me sternly, though looking gratified at the praise.

'. . . so wouldn't she follow?' I asked mischievously.

'No.' Matthew looked offended. 'She was quite rebellious really. I told her, *"How can we be a team if you keep losing the plot? I'm sorry to let you go, but it's for the best."*' He sounded like Sir Alan Sugar firing an apprentice. I began to think that there really might be somebody called Trixiebell. I could only imagine how delighted she must feel right now, having been dumped by Matthew.

'I like being free,' he informed me. 'Trixiebell and I weren't suited, but I think there may be other girls who would be more my type. In fact, there is one.' My whole being cringed at the possibility that it was me.

How could I wake Chloe up? Music! I leapt to my feet and lurched across the room. My groins were

155

still strained, but I had to escape into a Matthew-free zone.

'Oh, Matthew, you're in lurve!' I screamed, as loudly as possible, hoping the sound would rise through the ceiling and penetrate up to my bedroom, where Chloe lay. There was hope, although my bedroom carpet is very thick and expensive, as my parents constantly inform me whenever I spill nail varnish on it. 'We must have music to celebrate your romantic situation!' I roared weirdly.

I reached for the CD player, switched it on and turned the volume up to maximum. A deafening wave of classical opera came blasting out – Dad's into Verdi at the moment.

I saw Matthew's lips move, but I couldn't hear a word. This, though convenient, was kind of inconvenient, too.

'Sorry?' I mouthed.

'What?' frowned Matthew.

'You're in lurve!' I cried, wondering whether it would appear strange if, to celebrate Matthew being in lurve, I were to grab the broom and frenziedly knock it on the ceiling.

'Could we turn it down a bit?' Matthew was getting up. This was dangerous: I didn't want him roaming free-range round our kitchen, all amorous and sweaty. He might corner me by the microwave and who knows what might happen? Swiftly I turned the volume down slightly. But it was too late. Matthew was approaching me and looking deadly serious. I darted away and executed a mad Dance of Lurve around the kitchen.

'Matthew's in lurve!' I cried at the ceiling. 'It's wonderful! It's amazing! Congrats, old boy!' My groins were twanging with every step, but I had to keep moving. I know it's hard to hit a moving target, and I was hoping it would be hard to kiss one, too. Seeing Matthew's face closing in on you with his lips pouted would be like being frozen in terror halfway across a road and watching a runaway cement truck bearing down on you.

'I need to ask you something,' Matthew persisted, following me around and ignoring my strange dance and shrill celebratory cries. I had to stop this. I came to a halt on the other side of the table. He couldn't actually kiss me across the table, because, thank goodness, our kitchen table is blissfully wide. I'd never appreciated before just how wonderful wide tables are.

Matthew reached out and switched the CD player

off. What a bloody cheek! That was my CD player! How dare he come into my house and touch my gadgets without permission!

'Sorry,' he said, 'but it was doing my head in.' There was a sudden fierce prickling silence, in which I noticed that there was no sound whatsoever coming from the room above: despite my deafening pantomime, Chloe was evidently still fast asleep, the lazy old trout.

'Fine.' I shrugged. Matthew stared at me like a hypnotised snake. It was coming now: his declaration. It was *Pride and Prejudice* all over again: he was dreary and repulsive Mr Collins and I was Lizzy Bennet, and he wasn't going to take no for an answer.

'The thing is . . .' Matthew said, looking down at the table for a split second, 'do you think . . . should I tell her how I feel?'

'No!' I shrieked, a bit melodramatically. 'Not yet! I mean, observe her first.'

'I have been observing her,' Matthew said, observing me with horrid pale persistence, and visibly quaking like a pan of porridge coming to the boil. 'I've been observing her for weeks.'

'Her body language, Matthew!' I urged. 'What does it tell you?'

'I don't know!' groaned Matthew helplessly. 'I've

bought a book on body language but hers is really hard to interpret!'

'I know!' Suddenly I had a breakthrough. 'Let's ask Chloe! She's upstairs! Chloe is great on body language!' I danced out of the kitchen and headed for the stairs. And Matthew, that idiotic lump, actually followed me. I whirled around, trying to sustain my crazy delight. 'You stay in the kitchen!' I insisted. 'Finish your coffee! I'll wake her up and ask her to come down and advise you!'

'No! Wait!' pleaded Matthew. 'I don't want to disturb her, and between you and me, I don't find Chloe very . . . you know. *Simpatico*.'

'She bloody is simpatico, you liar!' I retorted in a desperate blast of mock frivolity. 'Go back and wait in the kitchen and we'll soon have this sorted for you!' And I ran upstairs.

Swiftly I hurled myself at my bedroom door. But it was, of course, locked. Oh God! *Where was the freakin' key?*

Chapter 18

My mind was a complete blank. The key! The key! The key! I felt in my pockets: nothing. What had I done immediately after locking Chloe in? I'd gone into Tam's room and tried on dozens of outfits. I raced in there. The floor was entirely covered in heaps of clothing, and her dressing table was unrecognisable under mountains of make-up.

I tossed the clothes about, looking for the key on the floor. I scrabbled among the lipsticks. Then I started looking in really insane places: in the bed, under the bed, on the ceiling. It is unusual for a lost key to be found on the ceiling, but I was desperate, and you never know.

I raced to the bathroom and searched on the window sill, in the bathroom cabinet, in the bath, in the loo. No sign of the key. Then faintly, from my room, I heard a feeble cry:

'Zoe?' Oh my God! Chloe had woken up.

I ran to the bedroom door and shouted, 'Hi, Chloe!' through it, trying to sound wacky and wonderful. Had she discovered the locked door yet or was she still blearily in bed?

'Zoe!' she called.

'Zoe!' That was Matthew, at the bottom of the stairs. 'Don't wake Chloe!'

'Too late!' I told him. 'She's already awake!'

'Zoe!' That was Chloe. 'Who are you talking to? What's going on?'

'It's only Matthew!' I told her.

'Who?' croaked Chloe sleepily.

'Paolo!' Matthew plaintively corrected me from below. 'Don't wake her up, it's not necessary. Tell her to go back to sleep.'

'It's only Paolo!' I shouted.

'Who?' Chloe sounded grouchy. 'Who's Paolo?'

'Matthew. You remember? He changed his name to Paolo,' I reminded her.

'Ugh!' responded Chloe with horrible clarity. 'That creep!'

At this point I staged a coughing fit to obliterate

Chloe's scornful insults. OK, Matthew was strange and khaki in many ways, but it wasn't necessary to say so to his strange khaki face.

Suddenly, disastrously, the doorknob rattled. Chloe must have got up and was trying to open the door.

'Zoe!' she cried, puzzled. 'The door's jammed!'

'No, er, listen.' I dropped my voice to a whisper. 'Just chill out for a min, OK?' Then I raised it to a roar, 'Matthew, go and make another cup of coffee! For Chloe!'

'I don't like coffee!' grumbled Chloe. 'What's wrong with this door?' She rattled and twisted the doorknob again. 'I think the freakin' thing's locked!'

'Does she take milk and sugar?' called Matthew.

'Milk, no sugar!' I commanded.

'I don't want any coffee!' snapped Chloe. 'Zoe, open the door! Why have you locked me in?'

'Shall I make her some toast?' called Matthew from below.

'No! Just coffee!' I was beginning to lose my rag with him.

'Zoe! I've told you I don't want any coffee!' snarled Chloe. She was losing her rag with me, and I didn't blame her. But on the other hand, I was beginning to lose my rag with her. I tiptoed to the top of the stairs and peeped down: Matthew had gone back to the kitchen. I heard him filling the kettle. I raced back to my door.

'It's just to get rid of him!' I hissed. 'I told him to make you a coffee so he'd go away and we can talk!'

'Zoe! Open the door! Why have you locked me in?'

'You were snoring in the night, so I moved to Tam's room, and I locked you in so you'd be safe from the murderous prowlers!' I explained hastily, glad that she couldn't see my face, which was bright red.

'I do *not* snore!'

'You so *do*!'

'Well, anyway, unlock the door! This is weird!'

'Chloe, I can't! I'm sorry! Listen, I can't find the key.'

'You *what*?' roared Chloe indignantly. This was a disaster. 'You lost the freakin' key?'

'I'll find it in a minute. When I've got rid of Matthew. He's distracting me.'

'What's he doing here anyway?' grumbled Chloe.

'He just – he brought some paintings round. For me to judge.'

'What?' Chloe exploded. 'Paintings? What paintings? What's going on? This is like some weird dream.'

'I decided to offer to help with Jailhouse Rock,' I gabbled guiltily. 'And this is what they asked me to do. There's a competition for kids to design the poster, and I'm helping with the judging.'

There was a brief silence on the other side of the door. Then I heard Matthew's footsteps in the hall below.

'Shall I bring it up?' he called.

'Noaw!!' I screamed. 'I'll be down in a minute! Just wait downstairs, Matthew!'

'Just one thing,' said Matthew persistently. 'Does Chloe take full-cream milk, skimmed or semi-skimmed?'

'Semi-skimmed!' I roared. I heard him go away again – in my present anguish, this was my only consolation. Ten seconds without Matthew was a major treat.

'Zoe,' Chloe's voice sounded different: not panicky any more, but kind of strange and hard, 'why didn't you tell me about this Jailhouse Rock stuff?'

'I forgot!' I flapped, trying to sound forgetful, but only as part of a bubbly fun package. 'Stupid of me!'

'You're lying,' said Chloe.

'OK,' I admitted hastily. 'I knew you wouldn't want to get involved with Jailhouse Rock so I kept quiet about it.'

'This is so weird,' raged Chloe, suddenly angry again. 'Let me out! You haven't lost the key! You've locked me in because you've gone mental!'

'I have lost the key! Just give me five minutes to find it!' I pleaded. 'Five! I promise I really have lost the key! I swear on the sacred name of Princess Diana!'

Chloe went quiet for a moment.

'You'd better find it soon,' she said menacingly, 'or I'm going to open the window and shout for help.'

'Don't worry! I'll be back in a minute!' I assured her, then ran downstairs. Matthew met me in the doorway, carrying a cup of coffee.

'Shall I take it up to her?' he asked.

'No!' I snapped, grabbing it. Some of the coffee sloshed out and burned my hand. 'She's not decent! I'll take it up to her!'

I carried the coffee upstairs. Matthew stood in the hall, watching. Maybe he was hoping for a glimpse of the indecent Chloe. Luckily the door to my bedroom isn't visible from the bottom of the stairs, so I crept out of sight, entered the bathroom and placed the coffee on the window sill. Then I went back down to the kitchen.

Matthew had made himself a second cup and was sitting at the table playing with a teaspoon. Oh my God! Maybe Matthew was the sinister midnight stalker! Perhaps he was planning to kill me with that teaspoon right now! I almost hoped he would. It would at least be a way out of my dilemma.

Hastily I made a brief inspection of everything on the window sill, looking for the key. No sign of it. Then I looked behind the toaster. Then in the knife drawer. Then in the cereal cupboard.

'What are you looking for?' asked Matthew. 'Can I help?'

'Only – the paracetamol,' I lied. I didn't want Matthew to know I had locked Chloe in. I couldn't come out of it well. I would appear either sadistic or incompetent. 'I've got a bit of a headache.'

'There's some paracetamol over there,' said Matthew, pointing towards Mum's little pill stash on top of the fridge.

'Brilliant! Well done!' I smiled brightly, getting the paracetamol down. What was I doing now? Taking pills when I hadn't even got a headache?

'Zoe!' There was a faint cry from upstairs. I ran out to the hall.

'I'll be up in a minute!' I yelled.

'Zoe! Help me!' called Chloe plaintively. I had to find that key. I raced back to the kitchen. Maybe it was in the fridge!

'What's wrong with Chloe?' asked Matthew, as I looked for the key in the butter dish.

'She's – uh, got a headache . . .'

'I thought you said you'd got a headache?'

'We've both got headaches, OK?' I whirled round accusingly.

'Ah,' said Matthew. 'I see . . . Uh – could I use your toilet?' I nodded, dumb and paralysed. I pointed upstairs.

'Second on the right,' I said.

He was going to go to the bathroom and see the cup of coffee in there! And Chloe was definitely going to call out, hearing footsteps on the landing. Oh my God! Could things get any worse?

I did the only sensible thing in the circumstances: I slipped out of the back door, ran down the path and hid in the garden shed.

Chapter 19

It was peaceful in there. In fact I thought I might stay quite a while – several years if need be. I sat on an upturned box. It splintered and I lurched to the right and struck my head quite hard on the wooden wall.

'Oh God!' I cried out in anguish. 'Why have You got it in for me?'

I stood up for a few minutes, but I felt so tired that in the end I found an old bucket of bulbs, tipped the bulbs out on to the floor, turned the bucket upside down and sat on that.

What if I never found the key? Would the fire brigade have to come and break my bedroom door down? Or would they rescue Chloe through the window on one of those long ladders? I cringed at the thought of my stupidity causing such a major emergency. What if Chloe got hysterical, tried to climb out of the window and fell to her doom?

That terrible thought made me leap up. I had to go back indoors and face the music. I had to get Matthew to break down the door. There was nothing else for it. He would despise me for ever, and so would Chloe, and my parents would be furious at the damage, but there was no alternative. I limped morosely up the path, heaved a huge sigh of trepidation and went back inside.

Chloe and Matthew were sitting at the kitchen table looking completely normal. Matthew was drinking coffee; Chloe, wrapped in my dressing gown, was sipping orange juice.

'Matthew got me out,' said Chloe, giving me a contemptuous look.

'The key was on the kitchen table,' explained Matthew. 'I noticed it while I was making that coffee for Chloe, so I put it back on the key board behind the kitchen door.'

Matthew had moved the key! And he'd hung it on the key board! Where all the household keys hang! I had never thought of looking there – because I knew that, even in a moment of temporary insanity, I would never in a million years hang it up in the proper place.

'Matthew's going in a minute,' said Chloe, with a meaningful look. 'He's been telling me about this girl he fancies.' My blood ran extra cold for a split second. 'But excuse me – I must go and have a bath – if that's all right?'

'Sure,' I said, leaning exhaustedly against the dishwasher. 'I think I'm going back to bed, because I slept so badly.' For a moment I was terrified that Matthew would offer to tuck me in and read me a bedtime story, but he just finished his coffee, wiped his mouth on the back of his hand in a way that was far from pleasant, and stood up. How wonderful! He was going. This was the best moment of the day so far – although, let's face it, there wasn't much competition.

I didn't really go to bed after Matthew left, because I knew that as soon as Chloe had finished her bath, there would be something of a showdown. So instead I slumped on the sofa and watched TV. I was shattered, and all my injuries were stinging and throbbing like mad, especially the latest one (the burnt hand from the spilt coffee). My eye was blacker than ever. I was planning to try and make Chloe feel guilty about that, if she was too hard on me about all the other stuff.

Eventually I heard her come out of the bathroom, and a few minutes later she appeared in the lounge and sat down in my dad's chair (if things had been completely normal she'd have flopped down beside me on the sofa). She had washed her hair and tied it back, and she looked strange and slightly intimidating.

I switched off the TV. Chloe stared at me and raised a very sarcastic eyebrow. My heart sank. I could so not face a row about this now.

'What on Earth was all that about?' she demanded.

'Look, I told you: you were snoring, so I –'

'No, not the locking me in stuff – the Jailhouse Rock stuff. Those paintings.' The paintings were still lying on the kitchen table, waiting for me to find the energy to look at them.

'Yeah, well, like I said: I've been helping with Jailhouse Rock,' I said simply and with a dash of defiance. I shrugged. 'It's not a crime. Everybody's helping. Jess and Fred. Toby and Fergus.'

'Why didn't you tell me?'

'Because I knew you'd be negative about it. Anyway, I only decided to do it yesterday.'

Chloe thought for a few moments. 'OK, I know I was against us getting involved,' she said. 'But you're entitled . . . I suppose . . . if that's what you want. But I still don't understand why you didn't tell me.'

'Because . . . well, I suppose . . . maybe because you've always been a bit weird about Beast.'

'Zoe, I've told you a dozen times, I am not weird about Beast,' she said firmly. 'I'd just rather not see him, and if you'd ever sent nuisance love texts to somebody, you'd understand how I feel.'

'OK,' I shrugged. 'But why don't you help with the publicity and stuff, too? It might be really good fun, and you might, kind of, get over the awkwardness.'

'No, thanks,' said Chloe firmly. 'It's not really my sort of thing. It's not what I want to do at the moment . . . Look, Zoe, I have to go home now, I'm sorry. I haven't even started on my Business Studies homework.'

'OK,' I said.

Shortly afterwards Chloe left. We hadn't had a row, exactly – we weren't even being frosty, but there was, perhaps, a slight chill in the air.

I spent most of the rest of Sunday looking at children's paintings. The competition revolved around jails (obviously, since Jailhouse Rock was in aid of Amnesty International). For the first ten minutes, the paintings were adorably sweet. For the next twenty minutes, they were quite appealing. By eleven-thirty, however, I was beginning to flag. By twelve I had looked at ninety-six paintings of people in prison and never wanted to see another painting of a prison for the rest of my life.

The ninety-seventh was different, though. This little kid had had the idea of combining the concept of prison with the fact that Jailhouse Rock was a rock concert. He (or she – the name was R Rogers) had drawn a guitar and the strings on the guitar had become the bars on a prison cell, and a prisoner was peering out between the bars.

It was so clearly the best painting by far that it was hardly worth looking at any more, but I knew I had to choose five, so I had to look at them all again. I selected the four that seemed to be the best. Then I started feeling sorry for the ones I hadn't chosen. Then I really did get a headache.

I went into the kitchen and made myself a cheese sandwich. Time was dragging on. I began to wonder when Mum and Dad would be back. I sent Dad a text asking how they were doing. How sad is that? If I were a cool goddess with street cred I would have organised a party in their absence, which would have been gatecrashed by five hundred people. Our house would have been trashed and we'd have got on the TV news.

I would, however, have been divorced by my parents so it might not have been all that fun, after all. I could have ended up imprisoned – in a guitar perhaps.

A reply came from Dad: **HAVING LOVELY LUNCH IN SUPERB PUB: ROAST BEEF ETC WISH YOU WERE HERE. BACK 4PM APPROX LOVE M&D.**

The sofa beckoned. After about ten minutes of *Heat* magazine I tossed it aside and closed my eyes. I was tormented by the thought that Beast and Charlie might be an item, and that Beast had basically not bothered to call by this morning but had just asked Matthew to come instead. Evidently seeing me was not high on Beast's list of desirable tasks, so the three centuries I'd spent getting ready to wow his socks off were wasted. I also had the threat of Matthew hanging over me. Surely it was only a matter of time until he made his declaration.

I was dreading seeing him on Wednesday at the Jailhouse Rock meeting, but I was also longing to see

Beast at the same meeting, so alternate waves of longing and dread swept over me for the next two days. At least having to wait would give my black eye time to fade and my grazes time to heal.

Chapter 20

Wednesday evening arrived at last. The black eye had faded to a tasteful yellow, and I had managed to hide it, and my chin scabs, with a thick layer of concealer. At the thought of seeing Beast, a flock of multi-coloured butterflies hatched in my tummy and performed a series of crazed pirouettes. I applied ten tons of cosmetics, wiped them all off and started again. I mustn't overdo the make-up. Beast would NOT be expecting to encounter a circus clown.

A horrid little chilly autumnal wind had sprung up as I walked along the high street, and a few pieces of litter were blowing about. The street looked desolate. The butterflies in my tummy evolved suddenly into a pack of mad dogs as I neared the building in which Beast was waiting. I came to the street door, which was open. There was a message pinned to it: *JAIL-HOUSE ROCK MEETING UPSTAIRS*. It wasn't Beast's handwriting. It was quite girly. It must have been Charlie's.

I tiptoed upstairs, my heart racing. Voices were coming out of a half-open door on the first floor: I stepped inside. Beast looked up. Our eyes met. The dogs which had been devouring my insides turned into a school of dolphins leaping across a glittering ocean.

'Hi!' I smiled, wrenching my eyes away from Beast's and politely smiling at everybody else.

'Hi, Zoe,' said Beast with a grin. 'You know Charlie and Paolo, er . . . this is Alex and Harriet. This is Zoe.' I nodded at the two new people: a fair boy with glasses and an amazing-looking girl with a thicket of dark hair. Maybe if Beast didn't go for Charlie, Harriet would be The Next Best Thing.

'We're just looking at the shortlisted poster designs,' said Beast. 'Have you brought yours?' I opened my bag and took out my five shortlisted paintings.

'I think this one's amazing – it's my absolute favourite.' I showed them the R Rogers one.

'Roy Rogers!' grinned Beast. 'A famous old cowboy from the 1950s. My role model.' I tried to smile bewitchingly, but it was hard to concentrate on what he was actually saying, as all my muscles were melting with joy at the sight of his restless grey-green eyes and black tangled curls.

Everybody looked at my five shortlisted paintings, and then I had to look at everybody else's. R Rogers's picture beat them hands down. Although the other people were slightly attached to their own best offers, they had to admit mine was in a different league.

'I think Zoe wins,' said Beast, giving me a smile. It wrapped itself around my heart like a silk scarf.

'Yes, it's brilliant, it's definitely the best,' said Charlie, kind of trying to take over the meeting. 'Shall we agree on this one, then?' she went on. 'I hate meetings that go on and on unnecessarily – I'm not really an ideal committee person. I like to cut through the waffle to what really matters.' I fought off a brief urge to punch her on the nose. So the rest of us were wafflers, were we?

'Yeah, this is definitely going to be our poster,' said Beast, looking admiringly at R Rogers's painting. 'OK, Zoe . . . uhhh, if you stay behind at the end I'll take you through what needs to be done next.' Beast flashed me a brief but delicious smile that turned my blood to champagne.

Beast wanted me to stay behind at the end! To tell me what needed to be done next! What needed to be done was for him to sweep me into his arms and let me rest my thudding little heart against his mighty chest. Then after that what needed to be done was for his lovely, pouty lips to approach mine . . .

'OK,' he said briskly, turning away. I bore it as well as I could. I did accept that he was going to have to look at other people occasionally, perhaps even talk to them. But it was diabolically cruel of life to be like that.

'Let's talk about the distribution plans – Paolo?' said Beast with a strangely restless sigh.

Matthew took a document out of his briefcase. I relaxed and tried to breathe quietly, although my heart was pounding, and my blood was bubbling and fizzing at the thought of seeing Beast on his own, afterwards. Matthew started droning on about his ideas for publicity. I couldn't concentrate for a while: the sound of Beast breathing was so much more eloquent than Matthew talking.

Eventually my head cleared and I managed to

listen. By now we were discussing arrangements for the concert itself. Beast leaned back in his chair, ran his fingers through his hair (oh, if only that was my job!) and shrugged theatrically.

'So . . . Rose Quartz. I've no idea what she's going to say next,' he sighed. 'So far we've had a yes, a no, another yes and a maybe.'

'She's just a spoiled bitch,' said Charlie.

'But we have to know whether she can be put on the poster or not!' Beast snapped. Charlie looked a bit hurt. I wondered what it was like to be Beast's PA.

'Well, there's no need to snap at me!' she said indignantly.

'Sorry, babe!' Beast reached out across the table and gave her hand a squeeze. *He gave her hand a squeeze and called her babe!* My heart sank. Oh my God! What if Charlie was going to stay behind afterwards, too? What if she was going to give me a secret wink as if to say: *I've got Beastie Boy tamed now, Leonie, or whatever your name is: he's realised we were made for each other?*

Now I was tormented again. It was exhausting, this lurve business. Although Beast had squeezed her hand, he had let go of it again right afterwards. But still, he *had* squeezed her hand! What did it mean?

Toby has squeezed my hand literally hundreds of times. He's hugged me practically every day for the past three years. But it means nothing, romance-wise. He's just a cuddly friend. Was Beast just being touchy-feely or was he smitten with Charlie?

Chapter 21

I watched them closely. Charlie looked secretly pleased with herself, but that was her usual style. Beast looked stressed out and preoccupied, but that was the way he'd been since he started to organise Jailhouse Rock. He was listening closely to Matthew – a triumph of concentration, as Matthew's voice is about as interesting as a concrete mixer grinding away.

They started talking about security, then ticket sales. Everything hinged on Rose Quartz being available.

'I think it's totally unprofessional of her,' said Charlie, tossing her head. Beast shrugged. 'She's being really mean to you.' Charlie looked at Beast in a way that was both challenging and sympathetic.

'She uses her sex appeal to get round men. I wish you'd let me deal with her.'

'OK!' Beast kind of exploded. It wasn't a major explosion, just a little quiet one, but Charlie looked shocked for a minute. It seemed this was territory they'd revisited over and over. A little electric moment of irritation seemed to pass between them. Maybe they weren't an item after all! Or maybe they *were* an item and this was a lovers' tiff. 'You deal with her from now on,' said Beast. I watched like a hawk, but body language can be really hard to interpret.

Charlie tried to look pleased, but you could see she was slightly anxious and trying to think on her feet.

'You can ring her right away, as we seem to be about finished here,' said Beast, pushing back his chair and collecting his papers. 'It's early afternoon in LA and that's where she is right now.'

'OK,' said Charlie, trying to sound capable even though she was obviously nervous. I mean, who wouldn't be, trying to ring Rose Quartz?

'You'll probably get through to her PA at best,' said Beast grimly. 'Or some clerk in her record company. It took me half an hour last time just to get through to her agent's secretary's secretary.'

'Fine,' said Charlie. 'Shall I call from our office?'

'Sure,' said Beast. 'I'll be up in a minute.' I was afraid that, once they were alone together in their office again, peace would be restored in a series of passionate clinches.

Everybody started packing up their stuff. Charlie went off upstairs. Matthew wanted to raise some dreary detail with Beast.

'Bye!' said Harriet and Alex, leaving with their lists of stuff to do. They looked happy. I heard him say, 'Fancy a coffee?' as they went downstairs. Ah, bless! I hoped they would fall madly in love. When you're in this crazy state you want everybody else to be, too.

'OK, Zoe,' said Beast, with a kind of sigh. Matthew's footsteps echoed in the stairwell. Somehow it intensified our aloneness. For me, anyway. He heaved another huge sigh, leaned back in his chair, looked at me and smiled. Sunshine seemed to flood the room even though it was actually dark outside.

'Phew!' said Beast, getting up, stretching and opening a window. 'Handling people isn't my strong point.'

'I thought you handled it all brilliantly,' I said, trying to sound light and airy and throwaway and not too adoring. In the room above we could hear the faint sound of Charlie's voice, starting her trans-atlantic phone call.

'It all depends on Rose Quartz,' said Beast anxiously. 'I hate celebs!'

'But she might have been having a rough time recently,' I said. 'According to *Heat* her aunt has breast cancer. It must be really tough, having paparazzi following you everywhere.' Beast looked thoughtful. 'You know . . .' I went on '. . . photographing you when you look worried, and selling those photos to all the magazines.'

'Hmmmm,' he mused. 'Well, let's hope she doesn't have some kind of meltdown, because we need to put her on the poster.' He picked up the winning artwork by R Rogers and studied it. 'Well done for finding this,' he said. 'Look at the brilliant way he's done the face looking through the bars . . .' This was an invitation to move closer to Beast. I could smell a faint scent, not aftershave or anything, but just the hint of summer rain and citrus. I think it was the smell of his skin. My heart started to pound.

'Look at those eyebrows,' he murmured, moving his fingers across the painted face. 'Sad . . . He's got it perfectly.' I wasn't looking at the painting. I was looking at Beast's hands.

I think the moment I fell for him, back in Newquay in the summer, was when I was looking at his hands, the night Tam had to go to hospital. His hands are so square and strong and beautiful. I'd longed to touch them then, and I felt exactly the same now. My legs started to tremble.

'Look at the way he's used the word "Amnesty" as if it's the make of guitar,' said Beast, with an appreciative smile. 'That's so clever. We'll get on to the school tomorrow morning and congratulate them. It's somebody in Charlie's mum's class apparently.' Charlie seemed to have her finger in every available pie. Her uncle ran Major Events and Matthew had told me that the reason Rose Quartz was willing to top the bill was that Charlie's uncle had been flat-mates with Rose's manager twenty years ago at uni. Charlie was unbelievably well connected.

'And the palm tree in the background softens the whole thing,' mused Beast. I wanted to stand here talking about the artwork all night, even though I was hardly looking at it at all. But eventually Beast gave a satisfied sigh, and handed it to me.

'OK, Zoe, what I want you to do now,' he said, resuming a businesslike tone, 'is to take this to the printer tomorrow morning, if you can. Drop it off on your way to school. I've got to go off at the crack of dawn to try and raise more sponsorship. But the printer is right around the corner from where you live. Gutenberg Printers, you know?' I nodded.

'Pete'll add the graphics and send us a draft copy for us to OK, and then we'll get them printed, I hope by the middle of next week.' Beast looked nervous. 'I have to get Rose Quartz to commit by Friday.'

'Beast!' Charlie suddenly called from upstairs. 'Can you come here a moment? I've got Nancy Schmidt on the line.' He was instantly distracted. Our moment together, which had been kind of private and almost tender, was over.

'Gotta go,' said Beast with a busy shrug. 'Thanks so much!' He was gone. I put the artwork in my satchel and went downstairs.

It was getting windy in the street, and I was happy it was dark. I walked along, heading for the bus station and enjoying the wind buffeting me – my heart soared like a kite. I felt like laughing and crying at the same time. On the corner of Wordsworth Street I met Jess and Fred. They were fighting, but laughing at the same time so it couldn't be serious.

'Hi, Zoe!' grinned Jess. 'How are you?'

'What's going on with you guys?' I asked.

'Fred's being a drama queen about going to the dentist!' said Jess.

'God!' I commented. 'If only I had a mere dental appointment to worry about. Men are such cowards. My dad's exactly the same.'

'So what's cooking with you?' asked Fred. 'Moving swiftly on from the dodgy topic of dentists towards what I hope is a real crisis.'

'I've just come out of a Jailhouse Rock meeting,' I told them. 'We're having the poster printed with Rose Quartz's name topping the bill, but will she show up on the night?'

'Oh, are you getting involved in Jailhouse Rock?' asked Jess. 'Brilliant! How is poor Beast? He was so stressed out about the poster design last time I saw him.'

'Oh, the poster's sorted,' I assured them. 'In fact, I've got the winning artwork in my bag right now.'

'Oooh, let's see!' demanded Jess. I opened the satchel and got out the artwork.

'We had a competition among the primary schools,' I explained. 'You know how amazing little kids' art is. I think this is absolutely –'

But before I could embark on my praise of

R Rogers's winning painting, a violent gust of wind snatched it clean out of my hand and it went soaring up into the air and away, over the rooftops of the distant houses and into the dark.

Chapter 22

'Oh my God!' I screamed. 'Catch it! Catch it! Catch it!' I raced off down the road – it was some distance before we got to a side street which would lead in the right direction. Fred sprinted ahead, although he is no athlete and his arms and legs were flapping all over the place. I could hear Jess puffing away just behind me.

'God! This is a killer!' she gasped. 'I've just had lasagne and chips!'

Down the side street and into the parallel road we ran: there was no sign of the artwork. Cans and crisp wrappers were blowing about. We raced up and down, peering into all the front gardens by the feeble light of the street lamps. We looked up into the branches of the trees, all swaying and creaking and bending in the violent wind. Nothing.

'It may have gone over into Byron Road,' said Fred, glancing up at the wild black sky. 'Come on!'

'No! Fred! Wait!' I panted. 'There's no point! It's gone! It could be miles away by now!'

We stood beneath a street lamp, gasping to get our breath back. The wind tossed Jess's hair about and tugged at Fred's hoodie. Huge anguish built up in my head. I was going to cry. I had lost the winning artwork! Beast would be furious. I would get the sack from the campaign. It would be the end of all my hopes. He would hate me for ever.

'What can I do?' I wailed. 'It's a disaster!'

'It must be somewhere!' said Jess. 'Someone will find it! Get them to make an announcement on local radio for everyone to look for it tomorrow.'

Right on cue, it started to rain.

'Oh no, no, no!' I groaned. 'This rain is going to ruin it anyway! I can't tell the radio people! I couldn't bear everybody knowing! Nobody must know! Least of all Beast!'

'Beast won't mind, surely.' pondered Jess. 'It was an accident.'

'He is fairly grumpy these days, though,' commented Fred dubiously.

Tears filled my eyes at the thought of Beast being disappointed in me. 'There's only one thing to do,' sighed Jess. 'You'll just have to fess up.'

'No, no – lateral thinking, my dear girl!' retorted Fred, putting on a posh professor's voice. 'What Zoe must do is forge a replacement.'

'Forge it . . . ?' I faltered.

'Yes, yes, you know what the original looks like, don't you?'

'Yes – right. It's a guy in jail, looking through the prison bars, but they're also the strings on a guitar.'

'Forge it, then,' repeated Fred. 'I wish we could help you but it is tricky to forge something you've never seen. Although I did get away with that Michelangelo last year.'

'It shouldn't be too difficult,' mused Jess. 'I mean, kids' paintings are always a bit primitive, aren't they? It's not as if it really was a Michelangelo or something.'

We parted. Jess and Fred promised to keep their eyes open for the artwork. I could hear them resuming their dentist argument as they strolled off down the road. I really envied them their relationship. They were mad about each other but really good mates as well. I bet they'll stay together till they're ninety.

If only I had a nice supportive boyfriend to help me through this crisis! I had a little cry on the way home, just to pass the time, and because basically I had lost the cherished artwork and there was no way out: Beast was going to despise me.

'Where have you been all evening?' demanded Mum as I entered the sitting room. I slumped down on the sofa next to Dad and let rip with another big salvo of tears. He put his arm round me. Mum switched the TV off and a sudden silence sprang up, punctuated only by my raucous sobs.

Between sobs I told the parents about losing the artwork. They looked concerned.

'You should ring them immediately and tell them what's happened,' said Mum.

'No! No!' I cried. 'I can't! I'll have to forge a replacement!'

'Good thinking, old boy,' said Dad.

'Jeremy!' snapped Mum. 'Surely you're not encouraging Zoe to cheat?' Dad shrugged.

'It just might be worth a try,' he said, eyebrows raised. 'It's a child's work, after all, so it's bound to be a bit rough round the edges. And anyway, you shouldn't be so high and mighty about it. What about that time at uni when you forged a letter to your tutor from your parents to say you'd had to go home for a family funeral? When we had our romantic little weekend away in Southwold?'

Mum blushed deeply, and though intrigued by the thought of their illegal tryst, I didn't want to hear any further details. With a cry of disgust I launched myself off the sofa, ran upstairs and gained the sanctuary of my room. My teddy bear Bruce waved gleefully from my pillow.

'Not yet, Bruce,' I sighed. 'First I have to forge a masterpiece.'

Luckily my childhood paints were stashed away untouched and there was some heavy-duty art paper under my bed. I blew the dust off it and cut it to size: A3. At least that much was going to be accurate.

I found the brushes, rinsed them in my washbasin and sat down at my desk. I closed my eyes and tried to conjure up the image of the winning design. But all I could see were Beast's hands.

When we'd been standing side by side, earlier, all I'd been aware of was the faint warmth of his body all down my left side, and the lovely square shape of his hands, and the citrus smell on his skin. I'd been completely and utterly oblivious to the painting.

Although I had looked at it earlier, of course, and

last Sunday, when I'd been drawing up the shortlist of five I'd been comparing it with the others all the time. But that was three days ago. And though I did remember the general design quite well, it was impossible to recall all the details.

The first one I did was way too small, I suppose because I was so scared. The second one looked like the smeary blotches of a toddler. The third one slanted off towards the left in a way that was unsettling. Halfway through the fourth one I began to feel desperately hungry.

I went downstairs. Dad and Mum were making their bedtime cocoa.

'I'm starving,' I announced.

'There's some chicken and salad in the fridge,' said Mum.

'Finished your masterpiece, then, old boy?' asked Dad.

'It's difficult,' I admitted. 'I don't know how they manage when they're trying to forge Michelangelo and stuff. I might have to fess up after all.' I addressed this remark to Mum to placate her a bit.

I went back to my room and recommenced the forgery. At one-thirty precisely I decided to stop. I'd gone dizzy with the whole thing, and I couldn't even remember what the original artwork had looked like. My latest effort, though lame and dire, would have to do. I would drop it in at the printer in the morning on my way to school, and hope nobody would notice that it wasn't the original.

Chapter 23

At school next day I was uneasy and preoccupied. I didn't dare tell Chloe that I'd forged the artwork, so I was trapped in lonely torment. Chloe was back on the goddess project, big time.

'I think we should call in at Baxter's on our way home,' she said. 'We could go to the beauty counter and get them to do a make-up session on us.'

I have been trying to get Chloe to think creatively about make-up for literally years. This was a major breakthrough.

'Great idea!' I patted her on the shoulder like a general congratulating his most heroic corporal. I needed to get into this, to force myself out of my artwork angst. 'Brilliant! We'd better call them first, though, and make an appointment.'

'You do that!' said Chloe. 'I'm useless on the phone.' I'd got my phone halfway out of my bag when I stalled.

'No, you do it, Chloe!' I insisted. 'Being so phobic about the phone is really holding you back. I'm not going to do any more phoning for you.' Chloe's eyes flashed, but she knew she was on shaky ground.

'This isn't for me,' she said. 'It's for both of us.'

'Well, for the past five years, whenever there's been any phoning of strangers, I've had to do the honours for both of us, and from now on it's your turn.' I grinned at her and handed my phone across.

Chloe took it reluctantly and switched it on. 'OK . . .' she mused. 'Oh! You've got a text!' Her eyes flared in astonishment. 'It's from somebody called Harry!' I grabbed the phone back. 'Who's Harry?' she asked.

'I don't know.' That was a stupid thing to say. As if I would get a text from a total stranger.

I read the text. **ZOE, PLEASE CAN YOU CALL IN AT THE OFFICE ON YOUR WAY HOME AFTER SCHOOL?** I deleted it swiftly.

'Somebody wanting to know Tam's new mobile number,' I lied, my face burning inconveniently. 'She's switched to a different network.'

198

'OK,' said Chloe. 'Let's get on with it, then.'

'Get on with what?' My face was boiling and so was my brain. The text from Beast had wiped everything else from my memory banks.

'I was going to call Baxter's and make those appointments, remember?' Chloe held out her hand for my phone.

'Oh yes,' I said helplessly. 'Of course.' I handed over my phone, and watched in dumb torment while Chloe first called directory enquiries to get the number for Baxter's, then faltered and flustered her way through to the beauty department, and then made two appointments for us after school, at the very time I had to go and see Beast in his office. I was double booked.

'Come on! Come on! Quick!' I urged Chloe, hustling her down the high street at ten past four.

'What's the hurry?' grumbled Chloe.

'I can't wait to see your new look.' I grinned treacherously. 'And I've just remembered I've got to see the doctist afterwards.' I would need an excuse to get away from Chloe afterwards, in order to see Beast alone.

'The doctist?'

'The dentist, the dentist.' We arrived at Baxter's and went to the beauty counter. A woman with very high eyebrows and a snooty nose looked down at us.

'We've got an appointment,' I said. 'For a makeover – make-up. Thing.' We gave our names, and she consulted some papers.

'Who wants to be first, then?' asked the snooty-pants.

'Chloe first!' I insisted, pushing her forward. 'While you're having it done, Chloe, I've just got one or two things I have to get for my mum.'

'Don't go!' wailed Chloe anxiously. 'What things?'

'Won't be a min!' I lied, and escaped through the handbag department.

Luckily Baxter's is a huge old-fashioned department store, so I was soon out of sight of the beauty section. I darted out into the high street and dashed to the Major Events office. Within moments I was in Beast's office. Unfortunately, so was Charlie. He was sitting at his desk; she was standing at the filing cabinet. They both looked at me in a way I didn't quite like. My heart gave a sickening lurch and went into car-chase mode.

'Zoe,' said Beast, looking mystified, 'did you deliver that artwork to the printer this morning?'

'Yes.' I blushed.

'Well, Pete sent us a mock-up for the poster this afternoon . . .' Beast pushed a printout across the desk to me. I looked down at it. There was my awful half-hearted forgery of the winning artwork, looking lame and poor. Pete had added all the words: the date and the venue and the starring artistes and where to buy the tickets.

'I just wanted to ask you, before I ring him, if this is the exact artwork that you delivered.' Beast looked into my eyes and, sadly, it wasn't a romantic kind of stare. It was more the kind of stare a weasel might direct at a rabbit seconds before pulling its head off. It was so obvious that he'd realised it wasn't the original artwork, but he wasn't clear about whether it was me or Pete who had messed up.

'Yeah,' I said in a tiny croaky voice. 'This is what I delivered.'

'But this is not that kid's painting,' said Beast. 'The guitar looks different, the face looking out is different, the stars are missing . . . I think Pete's been messing about with it or something.'

'And the word "Amnesty" is missing from the guitar,' added Charlie. I suddenly felt scared. If Beast accused Pete of messing up the poster design, and

201

caused a row between them . . . I shuddered. I couldn't get away with this. And poor Beast couldn't afford to lose any more time.

Beast was looking up at me, puzzled and stressed out. He didn't look furious – yet. But this was the moment when he would realise that I was, in fact, an imbecile. My eyes filled with imbecilic tears. Beast's expression changed from irritation to concern.

'What's the matter?' he asked.

'The wind . . . bl-blew it away,' I stammered.

'*What?!*'

'I met Jess and Fred on the way home,' I explained, a tear trickling down my cheek. 'And I wanted to show them it, so I got it out, and the wind kind of snatched it out of my hand and blew it up into the sky, and it went off over the rooftops, and we searched and searched for ages, but we couldn't find it anywhere. It was dark. I'm so sorry. I'm terribly, terribly sorry.' I ransacked my pockets for a tissue. Beast got up from behind his desk and came round to me. He put his arm round my shoulders.

'Don't cry, Zoe,' he said softly. If I hadn't been so upset, this moment would have been one to cherish. Beast's lovely citrus smell washed over me and I felt his breath on my cheek. But then Charlie came up to me, too, with a tissue, and kind of tried to join in the cuddle, grasping my arm and squeezing it. How dare she gatecrash our tender moment? I blew my nose and shook them both off.

'I'm sorry,' I said. 'I'm OK. I'm just so stressed out about the painting . . . I stayed up all night trying to make a copy of it, but . . . it was hopeless.'

'You should have told me, Zoe,' said Beast gently. 'It would have saved us a day. Pete's wasted time on this.'

'It doesn't look right,' said Charlie. If only a meteorite would smash into the office right now and pulverise her without touching either of us! But there's never a meteorite around when you want one. 'It's lost all the passion and the feeling, you see,' she went on, pulling a face at my artwork.

'Because you were trying so hard to get it right,' said Beast. 'It's the work of somebody who is trying to paint like somebody else. It would have been better if you'd just done a painting of your own.'

'No, it wouldn't,' I said. 'Because I'm rubbish at art.' This wasn't true, actually. Art is my favourite subject. But I was in a deeply penitent mode.

'We could use one of the other kids' artworks,' suggested Charlie.

'No,' said Beast. 'We've already told Ruby that she's the winner. I rang the school today to congratulate her. Funny, somehow I'd assumed it was a boy's work. Shows what a terrible old chauvinist I am!' He sat back down in his chair and searched through some random papers, whilst making a terrible groaning noise.

'Oh God!' I gasped. I was beginning to realise what it would mean to the little girl involved. I'd been so focussed on my own dilemma, I hadn't thought about the artist, at all. She was going to hate me for ever, too.

'The solution,' said Beast, 'is to go and see Ruby and ask her to do it again.'

'Oh brilliant!' gushed Charlie. She laid her hand on Beast's shoulder. He didn't respond. 'You are a genius, Beastie.'

Beastie! How dare she trivialise his magnificent nickname? He wasn't a pixie, for God's sake! I wondered briefly if she knew that his real name was Harry. *Harry.* Mmmm. I bet she did know it, though. She was the kind of person who'd ask you what star sign you were if you were standing next to her in a bus queue.

'And that's your job, Zoe,' said Beast. He found a

piece of paper and handed it to me. 'That's Ruby's address. Go round there, congratulate her, of course, and explain the situation.'

'Apologise –' added Charlie bossily. A meteorite was too good for that girl. Once I was a goddess, I was going to have to organise an alien abduction. She would be whisked off Planet Earth by things with slimy green tentacles.

'Zoe knows what to say,' Beast said slightly irritably. He wanted Charlie to shut up! This was the one tiny shred of comfort for me. 'Tell her we need another painting immediately. Ideally she'll be able to do it for you this evening, on the spot. If she does it in a hurry it might be a good thing. You know – capture the urgency, the feeling.'

'So you want me to try and get another painting out of this little girl *today*?' I asked, looking at my watch. It was already ten to five.

'Yeah, go for it,' beamed Beast. 'I'm sure you can work miracles. And ring me once you've got it.'

I left the Major Events office and looked at the piece of paper. Ruby's address was across town. I would need to get the number 114 bus. I was literally halfway to the bus station when I remembered, with a sickening lurch, that Chloe was still at Baxter's in the beauty department having herself transformed into a goddess, and I had to go through the same process before I'd be free to seek out Ruby and ruin her evening.

I turned and ran back to the high street and entered Baxter's. Chloe was sitting with her back to me while the beautician gave the finishing touches to her makeover.

'Your friend's here,' she told Chloe. 'Look at this transformation!' she invited me to admire her work. Chloe turned to me – she looked like a mad doll from a horror movie.

'Amazing!' I gasped. It's such a useful word.

Chapter 24

Half an hour later we were both mad staring dolls from *The X Files*, and to add insult to injury we'd been pressured into buying some horrendously expensive products so we'd be able to reproduce the ghastly look ourselves, at home.

'The one thing we should have bought was make-up remover,' I grumbled as we escaped into the public loos in the marketplace, and peered in anguish at ourselves in the mirror. 'We could have wiped the whole lot off straight away.'

'How could a beautician be so bad at her job?' frowned Chloe, with eyebrows that were several shades too dark for her redhead skin and permanently arched in a questioning way which was really unsettling.

'You know what we've learned today?' I mused. 'That we've got to be in charge of our makeover *ourselves*. We look atrocious. Like a couple of trannies. Now I'm going to have to go off and frighten the living daylights out of Ruby.'

'Ruby?' asked Chloe, puzzled. 'Who's Ruby?' It was time to tell Chloe the whole story of the lost poster. I explained, without referring to Beast, but saying that the Major Events 'people' were really cross with me.

'I'll come to Ruby's with you if you like,' offered Chloe. 'Give you some support?'

'No, thanks, darlin',' I sighed. 'This is my mess, I ought to sort it out by myself. And Ruby might be twice as freaked out if two of us turned up.'

'Especially looking like this!' giggled Chloe, pulling a sinister face beneath her two tons of make-up. 'Are you sure you don't want me to come?'

'I have to do this alone,' I insisted. 'It's only seeing a little girl, after all. You go home and make a list of new ideas for our goddess project – preferably revolving around cake and a sofa.'

First we took some photos of ourselves in our disastrous make-up – just so we could laugh about it later – and then we parted. I got the bus which would take me to Ruby's part of town. I was feeling really, really nervous. How do you tell a little girl that you've lost her prize-winning artwork? Especially if you're made up to look like the wicked stepmother in a fairytale?

I found Ruby's house easily, because one of Toby's friends lives in the next street and I went to a party there once. I felt very edgy as I walked up the path and rang the doorbell.

The door opened, and a smiley woman stood there. She had freckles and she was small and plump. She was wearing a nurse's uniform. This was Ruby's mum, presumably.

'Mrs Rogers?' I asked, trying to sound professional and cool, though aware that my make-up suggested a visit by some kind of Hallowe'en spook. She nodded. 'My name's Zoe Morris,' I said. 'I've come about the poster competition that Ruby won.'

Mrs Rogers frowned. 'What poster competition?' she asked, puzzled.

'Oh, haven't you heard?' I was surprised Ruby's mum knew nothing about it. 'Yes, there was a competition to design a poster for the Amnesty concert in December – you know, Jailhouse Rock. Maybe you've heard of it?'

209

Mrs Rogers frowned and shook her head. 'No, I don't think so, sorry,' she said. Beast had certainly got to improve his publicity. 'Come in, er . . . ?'

'Zoe.'

'Zoe. Sorry. I've had rather a tiring day.'

'Are you a nurse?' I was still trying to sound professional and cool. 'I think nurses are brilliant. I would love to be a nurse, but I can't stand the sight of – well, anything.' Mrs Rogers smiled.

'I'm a midwife, in fact,' she said, and led me into the sitting room.

A small girl with short, dark hair was sitting cross-legged on the carpet, watching *The Simpsons*. A rather faded-looking man with glasses was sitting in the corner working at a PC.

'Switch that TV off, Ruby,' said her mother. The dad swivelled round in his chair and gave me an uncertain smile. There was a sudden silence as the TV noise died. 'This is Zoe,' said Mrs Rogers. 'She's come about the art competition.' Ruby blushed violently. 'Zoe tells me you won. Is that right, Ruby?'

Ruby fidgeted uncomfortably on the carpet. Her face was scarlet. I felt really sorry for her, but mysti-fied. If I'd won an art competition I'd race home and ram the news down my parents' throats before they had a chance to catch their breath.

'Yeah,' she said, with a strange shrug.

'Why didn't you tell us, love? That's brilliant!' said her mum. Ruby squirmed and fiddled with her shoelaces. 'For goodness' sake!' her mum laughed. 'It's nothing to be ashamed of! Zoe says it's going to be on a poster – isn't that right, Zoe?'

'Yes,' I beamed, trying to banish from my memory the awful image of Ruby's artwork disappearing over the rooftops and into the night. The Rogers family had only heard the good news so far.

'But that's wonderful, isn't it, Dad?' exclaimed Ruby's mum.

'Terrific,' said her dad. 'Well done, Rube.' Ruby stared at the carpet and said nothing. She seemed really very shy.

'Would you like a drink, Zoe?' asked Ruby's mum. 'I was just making some tea.'

'Oh, thanks very much,' I stuttered, 'but there's something I have to explain first . . . It's a little bit complicated, I'm afraid.' A cloud crossed Mrs Rogers's face.

'Maybe we should sit down,' she suggested, sinking on to an armchair and looking apprehensive.

'It's not anything serious,' I assured them. 'At least, I mean, nobody's hurt, I mean . . .' I was getting stupidly flustered now. How could anyone get hurt on a piece of paper? 'The thing is . . .' I struggled on '. . . we were thrilled with Ruby's artwork, but unfortunately it got – er, damaged.'

'Damaged?' asked Mrs Rogers, looking irritated that her darling's work had been so badly neglected. Ruby just went on staring at the carpet. 'How?'

'Well, not so much damaged as lost,' I admitted, feeling terrible. 'You know it was very windy yesterday, right?' I went on. 'I was taking Ruby's artwork to the printer, and I met some friends, and I wanted to show them it, because it was so brilliant, and I got it out of my bag, and the wind kind of grabbed it and whipped it away, and it went flying off over the roofs.'

'Oh my goodness!' exclaimed Mrs Rogers. 'What a shame!'

Ruby looked up at this point and, curiously, her face cleared slightly, almost as if she was relieved.

'I don't mind,' she said, 'if you want to use somebody else's. Yasmin's was brilliant. It was loads better than mine anyway.'

'No, Ruby,' I insisted. 'You're the winner. We want

to use your design. All we need is for you to redo it.'
Ruby went pale.

'And because we're up against some terribly tight
deadlines,' I gabbled on, 'we were hoping you might
be able to do it right now . . . ?'

Mrs Rogers looked cross for an instant, then her
face relaxed.

'Come on, Ruby,' she said. 'Get up off that floor!
There's just time for you to do the painting for Zoe
before we have our supper. Dad, you can give me a
hand in the kitchen. Run and get your paints, Ruby.'

Ruby sidled off upstairs, and Mrs Rogers cleared a
space on the dining table.

'I'm really sorry about this,' I said. Mrs Rogers
tried not to look harassed.

'It's fine, Zoe, don't worry,' she smiled. 'It could
have happened to anybody. And it's a wonderful
honour for Ruby to win like this. Come on, Brian!
Switch that blessed computer off and come and give
me a hand with this supper!'

Ruby's dad abandoned his workstation and Ruby
returned with her paints. Her mum spread a news-
paper on the table first, and then her parents went off
to the kitchen. Ruby set out her paints and brushes
and a fresh piece of A3 paper, then she sat down. I sat

opposite her. She just sat and stared at the paper. Her face was a blank. I was really puzzled.

'Ruby, what's the matter?' I whispered.

She looked up at me with tears in her eyes. Her lip was trembling. Poor little kid! What on Earth was wrong?

'I can't do it!' she whispered, and two big tears burst from her eyes and ran down her cheeks.

'Yes, you can!' I hissed. 'Come on, Ruby!'

'No,' sniffed Ruby. 'I didn't do it in the first place. I cheated. *Don't tell Mum and Dad!*'

Chapter 25

'What?' I couldn't believe this. 'Ruby, don't cry. Tell me about it!'

'I couldn't do it,' whispered Ruby. 'I got stuck. Joe was home last week and he helped me. Well, he did it, really. I just did the stars and stuff.'

'Who's Joe?' I was already planning to track this Joe down and tie him to a chair until he'd reproduced the winning design.

'My brother. He's away at art college.'

'Oh my God! Joe Rogers! Of course!' I realised who Joe was. He'd been at our school, in the same year as Beast, but he was a quiet guy and I'd never got to know him. He spent all his time making sculptures and things, and he wasn't much of a party animal. 'You're Joe's sister! He's so talented!'

'Yes, well, that's why the painting won the competition. I never dreamt mine would win! I just got stuck with it and begged Joe to help me! I-I couldn't do it so Joe did it for me!' Ruby's face crumpled up in anguish. 'All this has happened to punish me for cheating!' Two more big tears slid down her face.

'Now, Ruby,' I whispered, 'you've really got to stop crying, because if your parents come in they'll find out something's wrong.' I spotted a box of tissues on the coffee table and handed her one. She wiped her eyes and blew her nose. 'OK, now can you remember what the design looked like?' I asked. Ruby shrugged.

'No,' she said gloomily. I felt frustrated. It was as if Ruby just wasn't trying. But I'd found it really difficult trying to reproduce the missing artwork, so how was Ruby going to manage it? And she wasn't in the right frame of mind.

'I can't pretend to be Joe pretending to be me,' she said hopelessly.

'No, of course you can't,' I said. 'Let's just sit and think for a minute. There's bound to be a way out of this.'

We sat quietly for a moment. Ruby just stared

sadly at the blank sheet of paper. My mind was racing.

'The concert's in aid of Amnesty, right?' I began. Ruby frowned slightly. 'You know what Amnesty's about, don't you?' She shrugged. 'In some countries people get put in prison just for saying things – for what they believe,' I explained. 'They haven't committed a crime. Here we're lucky, we can say almost anything. But in some countries you daren't even criticise the prime minister or you get thrown in jail.'

'My dad criticises the prime minister all the time,' said Ruby.

'Well, imagine what it would be like if some horrible men came in the night and dragged your dad away to jail.' Ruby pulled a tragic face. 'So that's what Amnesty's about. Helping and supporting those people in jail.'

'I remember now,' said Ruby. 'Mrs Jenkins explained it to us.'

'Well, think what it might be like to be in jail,' I urged her. 'The design doesn't have to be like the other one. Anything will do – as long as it's yours.'

Ruby heaved a big sigh and picked up the paintbrush. Tentatively, she started to paint. She painted some big prison bars, turning the piece of paper into a window.

'Brilliant! Brilliant!' I encouraged her. At this point her mum came in carrying a cup of tea for me.

'Well done, Ruby!' she beamed. Phew! Thank God she hadn't arrived a few moments earlier.

Ruby kind of stalled, once she'd done the bars, and stared at the painting.

'Will this do?' she asked.

'Er . . . I think it needs a little something extra,' I said, gently. So far we had prison bars: OK, it was a start, but it was hardly a prize-winning design. I could imagine other kids who'd entered the competition looking at it and bitching about how their design was much better.

'I know!' said Ruby suddenly. She didn't quite smile, but her miserable frown disappeared. She started painting little notes of music floating in through the prison bars.

'Brilliant! Amazing!' I encouraged her.

Ten minutes later it was all done. It was nothing like the original painting but it was simple, and really unusual. The prison bars looked grim and harsh, and the floating notes of music were multicoloured, like a flock of tropical birds.

'You know, Ruby,' I said, 'I think if you'd entered the competition with this painting you'd have won anyway.'

'Promise you'll never tell anybody that I cheated!'

'I promise. I think you've been punished enough!'

Ruby smiled, at last. As soon as the painting was dry, I left. Ruby's dad had found a big envelope to keep it safe, and I held it tight. The wind had dropped now, but I was still ultra-cautious.

On the way I rang Beast's mobile. It was on voice-mail. I tried to sound wonderful, but I felt so shattered it came out in a demented mutter.

'Hi, Beast, this is Zoe. Uhhh – you asked me to ring when the artwork was finished. It's nothing like the original, but I think it's OK. I'll drop it into the office tomorrow morning on my way to school.'

At last I arrived home. Dad was whisking up one of his culinary masterpieces.

'Sorry I'm a bit late, Dad,' I explained. 'I had to go to a little girl's house and get her to do a painting.'

'On your face, I presume,' he quipped, staring at my face with an amused expression. Oh God! The make-up makeover! I dumped my bag, placed the artwork carefully on the table and ran upstairs. The bathroom door was locked. I rattled the knob.

'What?' called Mum. 'I'm in the bath! I've had an awful day!'

My make-up remover stuff was all on my shelf in the bathroom. I went into my bedroom and looked at my face in my small mirror. The make-up made me look like a spinsterish businesswoman aged about forty. The sort of person who is trying too hard and has never had a boyfriend.

The front doorbell rang. I froze. I heard Dad go to the door and talk to somebody. Then he shouted from the foot of the stairs.

'Zoe! There's somebody come from Jailhouse Rock! About an artwork or something!' My heart gave a massive lurch. It was Beast! Oh my God! He mustn't see me like this!

'OK, OK, I'll be right down!' I called. Frantically I ransacked my room for anything which might remove make-up. I was tempted, just for an instant, to wipe my teddy bear Bruce across my face, but I didn't think it would give the desired result. The Baxter's beautician had used heavy-duty waterproof mascara. At least if I burst into tears, there wouldn't be any hideous smears. And this evening was turning out so stressy, I would almost certainly have to have a cry at some stage.

The thought of Beast seeing me in this god-awful

make-up would be enough to produce a deluge of tears of humiliation. I could feel them welling up right now and I hadn't even seen him yet.

With a huge sigh I nerved myself up to see him. I would tell him I was going to be in a pantomime, and I had been trying out the make-up for it.

'Zoe!' Dad called again.

'Coming!' I replied. I walked out of my room and arrived at the head of the stairs. But it wasn't Beast standing beside Dad, looking up at me. It was that infernal, interfering, prize-winning bitch, Charlie.

Chapter 26

'Hi, Zoe!' she called. 'I've come to collect the artwork. I thought I'd save you the trouble of dropping by tomorrow.'

I came downstairs, trying to hide my fury. She'd spoilt my chance of seeing Beast tomorrow. OK, I might not have seen him at all, and it would only have been a glimpse, but still . . .

'That idiot Beast left his mobile in the office,' said Charlie, following me through to the kitchen. Dad went out into the garden to pick some herbs or something. He's sometimes quite sensitive about leaving me private space if my friends come round. Mum hovers and eavesdrops.

'I heard your voicemail arrive,' Charlie went on, 'so I checked it in case it was something important.'

'Do you always listen to his voicemail?' I said, trying to sound teasing and lighthearted even though I was longing to pluck Mum's flowers from their vase on the window sill and smash the dripping stinky stalks right up Charlie's nose. 'You must be really close. Have you managed to tame the Beast, then?'

I picked up the envelope containing the artwork, turned and tried hard to give Charlie a taunting look. She smiled a horrid, secret, cocky smile. All my alarm bells started ringing so loud, it sounded like the Vatican at Easter.

'I think I have,' she smirked.

'Only *think*?' I tried to hide my desperation. 'Aren't you sure? Hasn't he swept you up in his manly arms and said, "*Charlie, you are amazing. I must speak to your father immediately*"?'

'Well, almost,' said Charlie. 'I managed to get through to Rose Quartz's manager and I insisted that we must have a decision, and somehow or other . . . I managed to convince them!'

Charlie was taking all the credit for this, but of course I knew the whole Rose Quartz thing had been possible because Charlie's uncle ran Major Events, and he'd been at uni with Rose's manager.

'So guess what! Rose Quartz has committed! She's on board!'

'That's great,' I had to admit. 'Beast will be relieved.'

'So relieved,' whispered Charlie, 'that he swept me up into a huge hug and said he didn't know what he'd do without me!'

My heart shattered into a hundred tiny fragments which went *tinkle tinkle tinkle* on to the marble floor of my soul. I was so tempted to tell her that Beast had hugged me once, too, out on the school field, when he was in a playful mood – that there was hardly a girl in town he hadn't hugged, especially a year or so ago when he was seriously into hugging everyone in sight.

I managed not to, though, because it was essential I mustn't appear to be a rival. Besides, the memory of that time Beast had hugged me was particularly painful, because back then I had hated Beast, hated every second of the hug, and when he hoisted me up on his shoulder and whirled me round and round, I had been mortified and enraged and desperate for him to stop.

I felt quite dizzy now at the memory of it. 'Well,' I said, 'don't forget to invite me to the wedding, because I have a weakness for insane hats.'

'Oh, Zoe!' sniggered Charlie. 'Don't be an idiot!' She squeezed my arm to indicate that I was, in fact, just the kind of idiot she liked. 'So I don't think I'm going to need you to find out what he thinks of me, after all! Isn't it amazing?'

At this point Dad re-entered the kitchen carrying a bunch of herbs and I introduced him to Charlie. Dad's always careful not to leer at pretty friends of mine, or say inappropriate things, but he has a certain smile which appears when he's introduced to some-body really gorgeous and he doesn't seem able to control it, even if Mum's around. I saw this smile appear now.

'Oh, a chef!' smiled Charlie flirtatiously. 'How wonderful! I wish I lived here!' I stifled the desire to attack her with the meat tenderiser. Not content with grabbing my heart-throb Beast, she was now seducing my dad!

'Oh, you wouldn't like me as a dad,' he assured her, moving rapidly away towards the sink. 'Zoe will tell you about my many disgusting habits.'

'No, I won't!' I assured him briskly. 'Anyway, here's the artwork . . .'

'Let's have a look at it, then,' demanded Charlie.

I pulled it out of the envelope. Her face changed. The twinkly post-flirtatious expression dropped away. She frowned. It was a maddeningly cute little frown, but welcome anyway after all that hideous leering at my dad.

'It's totally different!' she gasped. 'God . . . this is, like, not the same image at all. What is this, Zoe?'

'It's the winning artist's latest thoughts on the subject of Jailhouse Rock,' I said firmly. 'It was impossible to recreate the other image, and we think this one's better anyway. Much simpler.' I gave her a challenging glare. Charlie looked dubious.

'I don't like it nearly so much,' she said, giving me an irritated glance, as if I had seriously messed up.

'Well, it's what Beast thinks that really matters, isn't it?' I countered, in a sweet acidic tone of voice which made Charlie do a double take. Up till now she'd obviously regarded me as one of the other rather dull, identikit loser girls who floated hopelessly in her wake, like tiny rowing boats in the shadow of her magnificent cruising grandeur.

Now she looked sharply at me as if registering, for the first time, that I might actually stand up to her and offer her a bit of a challenge. Not romantically, of course, but in other niggling little ways which nevertheless, with any luck, could be irritating.

'You're right, of course,' she recovered, and slid the artwork back inside the envelope. She gave me a false, bright smile. 'Thanks so much for doing this.'

'No problem,' I shrugged, returning her gaze without flinching.

'Great new look, by the way,' she said, staring at my make-up. 'Kind of Forties Film Noir.'

'It's for a pantomime,' I said quickly. 'Chloe and I are doing a video of the ugly sisters, just for a laugh.'

'Oh, Zoe!' she simpered. 'You're not nearly ugly enough for that, even with that vampy make-up on!'

'Well, thanks for your vote of confidence,' I said. 'I'll try harder to be ugly in future.'

'You couldn't look ugly in a million years!' she trilled, patronising me now. She turned to my dad and fluttered her eyelashes at him.

'It was really lovely meeting you, Mr . . .' she faltered. She had forgotten our surname! She held out her hand.

'Oliver,' said Dad. 'I can't shake hands with you – mine are wet. Good luck with the concert. I don't suppose I'll be there. My appreciation of rock music stops with the Sex Pistols.' I wished he hadn't mentioned sex, or called himself Oliver (it's a family joke about Jamie Oliver, Dad's role model), but I was grateful to him for not shaking hands with Charlie.

I escorted her to the door. On the doorstep she turned, unexpectedly grabbed me and gave me a kiss on both cheeks.

'Thanks so much!' she breezed. 'You're a star!'

Having firmly put me in my place (servant), she flounced off down the path. I noticed her straight back. She was walking tall – well, she'd recently been hugged by Beast, so who wouldn't? I became aware that I was standing in a vile slumped posture which suggested a sack of potatoes. I shouldn't be watching her go, at all. Any minute now she might turn and wave. Hastily I started to close the door, and hey presto! She turned and waved just at the very moment when I had to peer through the door like a gothic retard, and I struck my hand quite hard on the door frame in my rushed attempt to wave back.

Game, set and match to Charlie, I thought, trudging miserably back to the kitchen with my head sunk firmly between my shoulders like some kind of grotesque subhuman from a *Harry Potter* movie.

'Well,' said Dad as I entered the kitchen. 'Who was that silly bimbo?'

'Didn't you think she was gorgeous?' I asked in disbelief.

'Oh, gorgeous in theory,' said Dad, 'but no man in his right mind would touch her with a bargepole.'

Although I've never been entirely sure what a bargepole is, I was grateful for this verdict, if mystified by it. I hoped that Beast would share Dad's reaction to Charlie's charisma overdose, but frankly, I doubted he would have the perspective. Dad likes women who treat him mean (Mum), but I was sure Beast needed all the cosseting he could get. And Charlie finally managing to get Rose Quartz to commit to the concert would have been a huge gold star in her already starry galaxy of attractions.

'I'm going to do my homework,' I said rather drearily. Dad didn't need to know it was two days' worth of homework, and that I'd forged his signature this morning to explain that the previous night's homework had been interrupted by a 'tummy upset'. Dear Dad! His ignorance of my intricate life made him somehow even more lovable.

They say that miserable women console themselves with food, and I was looking forward to my high-calorie supper in a way that was slightly ominous – it didn't bode well for the goddess project.

Chapter 27

'Well, we certainly learned our lesson yesterday,' said Chloe, as we strolled along the high street after school the next day. For a moment I wasn't sure what exactly she was referring to, since yesterday had been so crowded for me, I could hardly hold it all in my memory banks simultaneously.

'What lesson?'

'Getting some harpy from the beauty department to redesign us along the lines of a Bette Davis horror movie,' sighed Chloe. 'And she forced us into buying all that expensive stuff, too.'

'Yeah – especially as we're supposed to be saving up for our fabulous goddess dresses,' I sighed.

'How can we get the muns together in time?' Chloe grumbled. 'I'm totally broke.'

'Maybe we could borrow some,' I pondered. 'Tam owes me a couple of favours – maybe she can dig into her student loan.' However, I knew this idea was hopeless. Tam's more of a borrower than a lender – in fact I wouldn't be surprised if she called me this evening asking me to bail her out of some new financial disaster. It wouldn't be the first time.

'There's always babysitting,' suggested Chloe gloomily, even though she never babysits, because basically she's afraid of babies.

We turned into Market Street, and suddenly disaster struck: round the corner came Beast, carrying a pile of important-looking envelopes. My heart came flying out of my mouth, did two circuits of the marketplace and came to rest on his right shoulder, although he didn't seem to notice.

'Hey!' he grinned. 'Zoe! Chloe! How goes it, Chloe? Haven't seen you in a while.'

'Good, yeah,' said Chloe, looking a bit uncomfortable. 'How are you?'

'Oh, going mad, of course, but Rose Quartz is back on board,' said Beast.

'The Jailhouse Rock thing?' said Chloe. 'Cool! She's a legend.'

'She's also a pain,' sighed Beast. 'Never mind. I suppose she's entitled to be a prima donna.'

'Well, I can't wait to see her,' said Chloe. Beast turned to me.

'Zoe – the poster!' he said. 'I like it better than the other one. It's simpler. Well done! It's at the printer now and we should be able to start distributing it at the weekend. Are you up for that?'

'Uh – yes, I guess so,' I replied.

'Great. Well, I'll be in touch,' said Beast. 'Gotta go and catch the post.' He gave us a quick little wave, and was gone. I was expecting Chloe to say something edgy, but she smiled mischievously at me, which was a surprise.

'If only Beast would pay us to distribute the leaflets! I'd join the team right away.' She really didn't seem bothered by running into him, at all. I was the one who'd secretly imploded and was now a pile of singed feathers. I would have to come clean about the state of my heart to Chloe one of these days, especially now that she was clearly less bothered about seeing him. And anyway, since he was now apparently falling under Charlie's spell, Chloe and I were in the same boat: losers. Maybe we should form a grumpy little club and enjoy making bitchy remarks about Charlie. But first I had to come to terms with the idea myself: Beast and Charlie, an item? It hurt like hell.

Luckily this week coincided with a quiet patch on the Jailhouse Rock front. There were no meetings: we were all waiting for the posters and leaflets to become available as there had been some hold-ups at the printer.

I needed these few days anyway, to try and sort out my feelings for Beast. It was clear that he and Charlie were either an item, or about to become one. I desperately needed to get over him so I could struggle through the next few weeks without too much anguish. I was going to be seeing him occasionally: it was unavoidable.

I tried all the usual tricks. I imagined him sitting on the loo. He looked like a king on his throne. I looked up 'How to get over a crush' on the Internet. It was full of useless things like 'This person didn't ask you out: get over it.' But Beast had asked me out, last summer, and I'd rejected him in the rudest way possible. 'Get interested in somebody else' – that was another genius web suggestion. I watched the first of the *Pirates of the Caribbean* films, that joyous hunk fest. But, though Johnny Depp and Orlando Bloom are wonderful eye candy, they didn't cause dolphins to leap across my inner oceans as Beast did.

'Make a list of his faults,' advised the Internet. I got out a pencil. I wrote: *He used to think he was God's gift to women and would flirt with everybody in sight.* The trouble was, that was in the past tense. Beast *used* to be like that. Tam told me that when she was at school he'd been a famous serial love rat. But he really seemed to have changed in the last few months.

I tried to think of one thing to add to the list. *His nose is slightly crooked.* Big deal. His nose was, of course, crooked in a way which made all straight noses look rubbish.

The best method of getting over my crush, the only thing that worked, was imagining him with Charlie. Cuddled up on her sofa watching TV . . . Beast kissing her goodnight under a street lamp . . . running his fingers through her hair . . . I forced myself to watch endless steamy imaginary videos of him and Charlie getting up close and personal, and if nothing else, it did prepare me for what I strongly suspected was the reality of the situation. I had rejected Beast when he'd asked me out, and now I had to watch him romancing somebody else.

Charlie kept us all posted about the Jailhouse Rock

situation. She sent out texts with the latest about Rose Quartz. She was mildly misbehaving in LA; she fell over outside a nightclub in Hollywood and blamed the pavement; she attended a premiere dressed in a cobweb covered with raindrops; she got out of a cab and flashed her knickers at the paps. I suppose that was a good sign. At least she was still wearing some. It's always slightly worrying when celebs give up on underwear.

Although I spent ages peering at celebs' outfits, one of my biggest tasks was to earn enough money to buy my own. I decided to approach Mum. She was in a mellow mood after detecting a false insurance claim in Lincolnshire (that's her work, by the way, not some bizarre hobby). I made her a cup of Earl Grey and presented it with a distinguished Prince Charles Duchy biscuit.

'Mum.' I smiled persuasively. 'If I cleaned the house from top to bottom, would you give me £50? After all, you said I made a good job of the kitchen last weekend.'

Mum raised her eyebrow and bit daintily into Prince Charles's Lemon Crunch.

'Why would I do that,' she enquired, 'when every Tuesday Magda does it for forty?'

'But I'm your daughter!' I moaned. Mum dipped

her biscuit in her tea.

'It's a lesson we all have to learn,' she said. 'You can't buck the market.'

A couple of hours later I cornered Dad in his study. 'Dad.' I wrapped my arms round his shoulders (he was sitting at his PC) and attempted to strangle him with devotion. 'Could you possibly give me my Christmas present early?'

'I smell a rat,' said Dad, rather unpleasantly. 'What is this present anyway?'

'A dress . . .' I told him dreamily. 'The perfect dress . . .'

'You've got five thousand dresses already,' he said with a laugh. 'If you want it that badly, go and earn some money. Oh, there was a phone call earlier, from Jackie Norman.'

Oh no! The dreaded Norman twins! I would literally almost rather never see Beast again in my whole life than have to babysit for the Norman twins. Chloe used to come with me, but after the fiasco last time, which involved the twins peeing on us from a great height, we had vowed *Never Again*. I sighed. I knew I had to return Jackie Norman's call, at least. It would be rude not to.

I dialled the dreaded number. One of the twins

picked up. 'HARROW! HOARROW!' it yelled.

'Please could I speak to Mrs Norman?' I asked.

'HOOOOOO IS IT?' shouted the creature.

'Zoe Morris,' I informed it.

'It's ZAAAAAAAAAAWY!'

There was a brief but blessed pause. Then Mrs Norman picked up.

'Oh, Zoe,' she said, 'we never paid you after the last time you babysat for us – way back in the summer, I think it was – so we owe you £15. You must call by and pick it up.'

'Oh yes! Thanks,' I said. 'I'll drop by.' Surprisingly, she didn't ask me to babysit, so I emerged unscathed from a call I'd been dreading.

£15 wasn't much, but it was a start. I had to have that dress. And if Beast was going to be Charlie's squeeze from now on, I would at least be able to take his breath away for a split second, and make him realise what he was missing. I so *had* to have that dress.

Five minutes later, the phone rang again.

'Hi,' droned a familiar voice. 'This is Paolo. Great news! The leaflets have arrived and you're leafleting with me tomorrow.'

Great news indeed. Leafleting with Matthew. I could hardly wait.

Chapter 28

I met Matthew by the Catholic church. He was carrying a heap of leaflets.

'Hi, Matthew!' I smiled briskly, as if to indicate that we would not be spending time together at all if it wasn't for our task. This was work, not a date, and certainly not the moment to ask me out after his nerve had clearly failed him last Sunday morning.

'Paolo,' he corrected me.

'Paolo, of course. Sorry, Matthew.' I grinned, taking the piss slightly.

'Hi,' he droned with a slight frown. 'Let's rock.' He was still using the faux cockney accent.

'Hardly my idea of rocking, but let's see the handouts anyway.' They were a smaller version of the posters: Ruby's design looked great, and Rose

Quartz's magical name was blazed across the top in pink glittery letters. 'Awesome!'

We set off down Longville Street, going up alternate front paths. At the bottom of the street we paused while Matthew got some more leaflets out of his shoulder bag. So far it had been relatively painless.

'Beast must be relieved now the publicity's out and Rose Quartz is up for it,' I said, to make conversation while Matthew fumbled with the buckles on his bag.

'Oh yes,' he nodded solemnly. 'Beast's a happy bunny now, yes siree!' Matthew's choice of words was bizarre, but I detected something nasty behind it.

'A happy . . . bunny?' I repeated faintly, peering at his strange pasty face for further clues.

'Mustn't say anything, sworn to silence, but the ladies do seem to confide in me.' He gave me a weird louche wink.

'What do you mean?' I begged. 'What ladies?'

'Well, you know yourself, there are certain guys who girls naturally feel relaxed with,' said Matthew, handing me a pile of leaflets. 'Guys, well, like a kind of gay best friend, only not gay.'

'I know,' I said. 'I've got Toby,' I added firmly, so Matthew would clearly understand there were

No Vacancies as far as I was concerned.

'Well, I'm a bit like that,' Matthew went on. We set off towards Newton Road. 'Girls tell me their secrets.'

'Who's been telling you their secrets?' I pestered him. 'Charlie?'

Matthew gave a horrid secret grin and slid a lizard-like look my way. 'Hmmmm, you're on the ball today, Miss Zoe,' he said, sounding like Cary Grant in a 1950s movie: not quite British, but not quite American, either. Sadly, Matthew did not look like Cary Grant, more like an aardvark, although he lacked the aardvark's cute perky ears. 'You may have thought I had a bit of an – erm, crush on Charlie when I told you about her last Sunday.' What? My ears pricked up, big time. I was the aard-vark now.

Matthew had been talking about *Charlie* last Sunday! He hadn't been hitting on me at all! Whilst feeling immensely relieved that I was not Matthew's lurve object, I was also somehow rather insulted and annoyed that it was Charlie – such a cliché.

'You gave me the right advice,' droned Matthew. 'You told me not to say anything and to watch her body language. And I was watching her body

241

language a couple of days ago and she started talking about Beast, and that's when I realised . . . well, I didn't really fancy her that much anyway.'

'What did Charlie say about Beast?' I persisted, as we delivered leaflets in a synchronised manner to Number 105 and 107 Newton Road. It was a Victorian terrace, so we were able to continue our conversation as we walked up adjoining paths.

'Oh, various little secrets . . .' He smiled to the path. My heart lurched sickeningly. I had deeply suspected that Charlie and Beast were an item, or likely to be, but maybe now I had to take it on the chin: Matthew could provide confirmation.

'Don't tell me she's Beast's latest squeeze?' I tried to sound scornful and dismissive, as if Beast had a different squeeze every week. My own heart squeezed in anguish at the thought of Beast squeezing Charlie.

Matthew stopped in his tracks, halfway up the path to Number 109.

'How did you know?' he asked.

'Oh – it's obvious,' I shrugged, stuffing a leaflet through a letterbox, whilst silently my entire being unravelled into dust. It was over for me: Beast and Charlie were together. I had in some way essentially died whilst actually mysteriously remaining alive. My legs kept carrying me up and down paths, my voice kept making conversation, even perky conversation, but my eyes were as dead as a zombie's and my brain had become a dark drizzle. Come to think of it, I was now the perfect match for Matthew.

'She's amazing,' I said, privately thinking how amazingly naff she was.

'All girls could take a leaf out of Charlie's book,' intoned Matthew solemnly. I thought that I would like to take a leaf out of her book and shove it down her throat. 'Don't take this the wrong way, Zoe, but I think you could learn a bit from Charlie.'

'Oh?' I enquired archly, infuriated by his ponderous rudeness. 'How exactly?'

'Well, everything, really; the way she moves . . .' I made an instant plan to see how she moved when a rhinoceros was chasing her; I was going to organise it, no problem. 'The way she dresses, her perfume . . . The way she treats a guy.'

'How does she treat a guy?' I demanded sulkily, and no doubt unattractively.

'She makes him feel like a king,' sighed Matthew. 'She even told me that if it hadn't been for Beast, she would have loved to go out with me.'

I was silenced by the monstrosity of Charlie's lie,

but impressed at her sheer devotion to the task of making everybody love her – even Matthew.

'I hope you don't mind me saying this, Zoe,' said Matthew, stopping for an instant and staring morosely at me over a grubby hedge. 'But I do think Charlie can teach you a thing or two.'

'Of course I don't mind!' I shrieked, thirty seconds from murdering him. 'I'm totally into self-improvement, as you know! It's my big project with Chloe this autumn! And if you remember, I was your life coach once!'

'Yes.' Matthew suddenly seemed to remember how we'd met: he'd answered our advert when Chloe and I had been pretending to be life coaches for some reason too embarrassing to recall. 'You were wrong about brown, though,' he told me reproachfully. 'Charlie put me right about that.'

'Is that why you're wearing that colour?' I asked. 'What is it – wet toad or frozen mud?'

'This is taupe,' said Matthew proudly. 'Charlie told me you can't go wrong with taupe.'

'Well, Matthew,' I stopped in my tracks for an instant, 'though I'm delighted you've found another style advisor, and clearly gone way upmarket, I'm sorry to have to tell you that you never paid your bill, and that, in fact, you owe me thirty quid.'

He may have unwittingly broken my heart and destroyed my self-confidence, but by heaven the prat was going to pay for it.

Chapter 29

Matthew argued feebly for a couple of minutes. Secretly I knew it wasn't really his fault: after all, I'd failed to send him an invoice, but he didn't know that. I pretended I had sent one, and in the end he rather surprisingly handed over the £30 there and then.

After delivering another six billion leaflets, we parted. I went back to the town centre and walked about a bit, fuming at the thought of Charlie being able to 'teach me a thing or two' as Matthew so tactlessly put it. How dare Matthew compare me unfavourably with that simpering bimbo? How dare she pull Beast? How dare Beast let himself be seduced by her? I hated them all!

I quite liked the feeling of hate. It seemed to come

with a free energy surge. So Beast and Charlie were an item? Who cared? All that mattered to me now was my sizzling pink dress. I was going to turn up at Jailhouse Rock looking like a million dollars, and Beast would feel his heart crack right down the middle. But it would be too late. Hah! Serve him right!

The dress was still there, waiting for me. I told them I could add another £30 to the fund, and handed over the £30 Matthew had just paid me. Then I tried the dress on again. It was better trying it on without Chloe, because having a best friend who's skinny is fine in most situations, but when you're in a changing room together, sometimes daylight mysteriously turns into the blackest darkness.

Holding my breath (I hadn't lost much weight yet), I could see that the dress was still working its magic. It looked like me wearing it, but a better, five-star version of me: my skin glowed and the dress coaxed my rather random flab into stylish curves.

'I'll be able to pay the rest in a couple of days,' I promised the assistant, handing the dress back.

I decided to walk home, even though I'd already pounded the pavements with Matthew for a couple of hours. I bought a bottle of water from the newsagent, but ignored the chocolate bars. Charlie could teach me a thing or two indeed! *I* was going to teach *her* a thing or two.

On the corner by the cybercafe I met Jess and Fred. They grabbed me.

'We've seen the poster!' enthused Jess. 'It's a triumph!'

'You're a genius!' added Fred. 'We want you to mastermind the poster for our first world tour!'

'OK, OK,' I grinned. 'But I must warn you that my rates are £5,000 an hour.'

'Of course, of course.' Jess waved the subject of money grandly away. 'Please discuss all those sordid details with our agent.'

'Who is your agent?!' I enquired.

'Frog and Nightgown,' said Fred.

'Slug and Lettuce,' retorted Jess.

'Hare and Hounds,' quipped Fred. These were, of course, the names of pubs, not agents.

'George and Dragon,' insisted Jess. 'George does the schmoozing, Dragon negotiates the deals.'

'Well, you can tell Dragon I'll be in touch in the morning, then,' I informed them. It was great to be talking to Jess and Fred. They are so life-enhancing.

'So what's the latest on your brilliant careers, *really*?' I enquired.

'Well, Beast has given the OK to our sketch for Jailhouse Rock,' said Jess.

'What's it about? Let me see it!'

'No, no!' Fred staged a panic. 'Not in the high street! It might cause a scene!'

'Actually, we don't really want anyone to get a preview, Zoe – no offence – it's just that we feel a bit superstitious about it. We want to keep it under wraps until the night.'

'Sure, sure, of course, I understand,' I assured them.

'But on the other hand . . .' Jess looked anxious. 'We're both suffering horribly from nerves!'

'It's terrifying,' Fred added. 'If it wasn't for Amnesty, we'd run away to South America.'

'Plunkett is such a massive venue,' shuddered Jess. 'It must hold, oh . . .'

'. . . seven billion.' Fred shook his head in serious fright.

'And we haven't had enough experience!' whimpered Jess.

'You've done assemblies at school. And that end-of-term comedy show you did – with the

Olympics – was hilarious.'

'Yes, but that was in front of our friends. What we need is a couple of gigs where we perform to strangers.'

'But I thought you said you wanted to keep it under wraps?'

'Oh, I don't mean we want to perform our sketch for Jailhouse Rock: just other stuff, anything to anybody. Just a bit of experience, performing to strangers. I mean, we've got loads of sketches. We write them all the time.'

'We've written a couple just now, while we've been talking to you,' Fred informed me in an offhand way.

I promised them that if I met any strangers who needed entertaining, I would swiftly organise a gig for them, and with a few more quips, we parted.

It had been great talking to Fred and Jess, but I realised how glad I was that I wasn't required to get up on stage at Plunkett. All I had to do was be fabulous in the audience. And boy, was I going to be fabulous! I didn't know where all this buzzing energy had come from, but it was probably wounded pride and a broken heart. Still, it sure beat moping about and weeping into Bruce the Bear for seven hours. (My normal routine.)

I strode along with the air of a Tyrannosaurus rex – or maybe that should be Tyrannosaurus regina. I felt kind of liberated. So Beast was with somebody else? So what? It was as if I'd somehow got out of jail.

On the way home I called at the Normans' house. Jackie opened the door.

'Oh, Zoe, yes – that £15 we owe you,' she said. 'In fact, we've kept you waiting such a long time – let's call it twenty.' I didn't argue, but just protested politely for a moment or two, then accepted with effusive thanks.

'Zoe, you couldn't babysit for us on the twenty-fifth, could you?' said Jackie suddenly, as if it had just entered her head, but I now realised I'd been set up. 'We can make it £20 on a regular basis if you like,' she added. My first reaction was to cringe at the very thought of the twins, back down the path and run away like mad. But then something odd happened. I felt a surge of rebellious energy.

'Yeah, OK,' I was astonished to hear myself say, but I seemed to have grown a backbone in the last couple of hours. No way was I going to be intimidated by a couple of tiny little kids, no matter how feral.

'Oh, Zoe, could you?' Jackie reached out piteously

and clung gratefully to my sleeve, like a beggar touching a princess. In strict financial terms, of course, the roles were reversed, but I held all the aces: I didn't *have* to spend any time at all with her loathsome offspring, whereas she was stuck with them for eternity. I could hear them screaming somewhere upstairs.

'Our Polish girl's leaving,' said Jackie ruefully, pulling a guilty face. 'Her mother's ill. She's got to go back to Kraków.' Either the Polish girl was lying, or Jackie was lying: we both knew the reason the girl was fleeing wasn't her sick mother. It was the twins' monstrous misbehaviour.

'I didn't know you had a Polish girl,' I said.

'Oh yes,' Jackie sighed. 'She's only been with us for a few weeks. We were hoping she'd stay till next spring, but . . .' Upstairs there was the sound of galaxies being destroyed.

Was I out of my mind, willingly volunteering to expose myself to these tiny monsters again? No, I was not. I was going to tame them. It was like some epic challenge: The Lord of the Twins. We swiftly agreed the details for my forthcoming visit and parted. I put the £20 into a special zipped section of my wallet: the sizzling pink dress fund.

I entered my own home with explosive power and surged into the kitchen. Mum was staring dolefully into the fridge.

'No fatty food for me from now on,' I informed her. 'Salads, fruit, protein, nuts and seeds.' Mum looked startled. 'Sorry,' I added. 'I should, of course, have said "*Good evening, Mother. How was your day?*"'

Mum closed the fridge door and approached me warily, her eyes fixed anxiously on my face.

'You haven't . . . been taking drugs, have you, Zoe?'

'Certainly not!' I snapped. 'You're the one who takes the drugs in this house, remember? All those indigestion pills? The paracetamol on top of the fridge?' Mum looked guilty.

'Chicken salad all right, then?' she asked.

'Perfect!' I replied. 'I'm going to get into shape. Homework now, OK?' Mum nodded. I ran upstairs to my room.

I would have expected myself to burst into tears at this moment. I knew, now, that Beast and Charlie were an item. I had been insulted by Matthew. My world had crashed and burned. But strangely, I had never felt further from tears. I was still full of that weird energy that had seized me earlier. I threw open my wardrobe door and scowled at my clothes.

'Be afraid!' I warned my clothes. 'Be very afraid!' I grabbed my digital camera.

Two hours later, seventy-five per cent of them were for sale on eBay.

Chapter 30

'So,' I told Chloe next day as I munched my tuna salad at lunchtime, 'I've cleared out my wardrobe and I've got loads of stuff for sale on eBay. Plus I've called in a couple of debts. I'll soon have that dress paid for and on my back.'

'My dad gave me some money for mine,' said Chloe, looking a bit guilty.

'Wow! Lucky!'

'I will clear out my wardrobe soon, though,' said Chloe thoughtfully, carving up her baked potato. 'I do need to get rid of stuff.'

'No you don't, if you don't want to,' I told her. I was still full of that weird energy I had acquired whilst delivering leaflets with Matthew.

'But when you looked through my wardrobe, you

said I should chuck out . . .' Chloe's voice trailed away and she gave me a puzzled stare.

'You don't have to get rid of anything if you don't want to, babe!' I assured her. 'The Hammy T-shirt, the tortoises . . . keep the lot. You'll have a little girl one day and it can be her heritage collection.' Chloe looked relieved.

'I think I will keep them, actually,' she said. 'There's no harm in it. We don't have to do things because . . . well, just because we decided to.'

'We can change our minds!' I beamed at her. It wasn't rocket science. But it felt like some kind of revelation. I was feeling better about things now. The only blot on the horizon was having to babysit for the Norman twins. I'd agreed to it in a weird heroic mood, but I kept being haunted by memories of the previous humiliations those horrid little boys had imposed on me.

Later I met Jess and Fred in the science quad. They were arguing about a packet of crisps.

'Hi, guys!' I called. 'How's it going?'

'Oh, hopeless,' said Jess. 'We keep changing our minds about the sketch for Jailhouse Rock. Fred's always coming up with these new ideas.'

'Sorry.' Fred hung his head in mock shame. 'Apologies for my brilliance. I am on the waiting list for a partial lobotomy, but till then – you'll just have to put up with my genius.'

'And we haven't had a chance to practise in front of anybody,' grumbled Jess, scrunching up the crisp packet. 'We don't want to perform in front of our friends because we know they won't be objective, they'll just kind of go, "*Darlings, you were wonderful.*" But we won't get any really helpful feedback.'

'Oh well,' I shrugged. 'Apart from that, life is OK? You haven't been mugged or anything? No operations scheduled?' They had a great career in front of them, and they had each other: I was so jealous of them. If Beast and I were together I'd be in five-star heaven and I'd never grumble about anything minor, ever. For a split second I felt a stab of agony at the thought that Beast's arms might at this very moment be wrapped around Charlie. Jess peered at me.

'Zoe, what's wrong?' she asked.

'Oh, nothing.' Hastily I shook off my horrid hallucination. 'It's just – I'm dreading . . .' I ransacked my memory banks for something to dread. 'Babysitting!' I exclaimed. 'I have to babysit for these two little horrors. The Norman twins. They're vile. Last time I went they trashed the house and I had a nervous breakdown.'

'How old are they?' asked Jess.

'Err . . . three? Four? Not sure. Preschool.'

'Preschool? But that's tiny! We'll give you a hand, Zoe. Won't we, Fred?' Fred looked wary and shrugged. 'When is it?' Jess went on.

'Next Saturday,' I told them.

'We'll be there!' Jess assured me, squeezing my hand. 'We'll outnumber them! We'll terrify them!'

'And we'll tell them that if they don't behave, we'll perform our sketch show to them,' added Fred. Jess turned to him, an idea visibly dawning on her.

'We could perform anyway!' she said, suddenly grabbing him. 'Why not? That animal stuff we were working on, for a children's show!'

'I was thinking more in terms of a whole play-group,' said Fred doubtfully. 'Not an audience of two.'

'It'll be three with Zoe!' Jess insisted. 'And anyway, we can try stuff out without it being so scary as a whole class! We're doing it, Parsons – complain at your peril!' Fred pulled a henpecked sort of face. 'If you don't go along with it, we're finished! I shall go back to Ben Jones!' Jess was laughing as she delivered this threat, but you could see she was serious, although she's never been out with Ben Jones. However, Fred seemed to understand that she wasn't to be trifled with.

'OK,' he said. 'We're on. Our agent will be in touch about the fee.'

Jess and Fred agreed to make their show fragrant and child-friendly and went off discussing which animal sketch might be best.

'In my next life,' Fred was saying, 'I'm going to be a parasite.'

'You already are!' Jess replied. 'You owe me ten quid, remember?'

In my next life I was going to be a goddess. But my next life had started already. It was so weird: I'd wanted to become a goddess in order to sweep Beast off his feet, and the moment I realised he wasn't available, I'd kind of become a goddess anyway.

As I walked home I had a think about the way things had changed. OK, Charlie and Beast were an item, and it hurt like mad. But instead of feeling sick to my stomach, limp and tragic, I had become angry. I think it was because Matthew had served it up to me, and added all that insulting stuff as a side dish:

how Charlie could teach me a thing or two, and how wonderful she was.

To hell with Charlie! I didn't need a role model. I wasn't ever going to be remotely like Charlie, and I was glad. Let Beast flirt with her all day if that was what he wanted. I had started off last year by hating Beast and I was pretty sure I could get back in touch with those old feelings again if necessary. I think what I was going through was a severe attack of sour grapes, but it felt OK. It felt quite exhilarating.

'I don't care if I never have a boyfriend,' I told Chloe next day. I was feeling even more determined and liberated. I'd been imagining Charlie and Beast's future lives together. They already had three screaming kids, she'd lost her looks and he'd become a paunchy couch potato. I, meanwhile, had become a top designer with offices in New York, London and Paris, with a beautiful Brazilian assistant called Luis Quango, who exercised my deerhounds every morning in Central Park. Beast read about me occasionally in the newspapers, and shed a regretful tear.

'I don't care if I don't, either,' said Chloe hastily. 'I've always said so, right at the start of this term, when we decided we were going to become goddesses and stuff. I said it wasn't going to be about boys. Boys are off the radar.'

'And they can stay there,' I added firmly. I wasn't going to have to tell Chloe that I was mad about Beast. That was a huge relief. I hadn't realised just how much I'd been dreading coming clean to her. Maybe that was why I was filled with this weird buzzing energy, nowadays.

However, there were more demons to face on the evening of the twenty-fifth. Last time I babysat the Norman twins, it had ended in mayhem. They'd been so vile, I'd vowed I'd never ever babysit for them again. But was I going to allow myself to be beaten by a couple of piddling little kids? No way. I prepared very carefully for the evening, dressing in fierce black and red, and giving myself very frightening eyebrows.

'They're not asleep, I'm afraid,' Jackie Norman whispered guiltily as she let me in. The twins thundered downstairs, in their pyjamas, but about as far from sleep as mammals have ever been.

'Zaaaaaooowy! Zoooooowy!' they yelled. They grabbed my legs. Usually at this point they dive under my skirt in a quest to see pants, but I wasn't that stupid. I was wearing black drainpipe jeans. They tugged at my belt, roaring in their usual manner.

'Stop that, boys!' snapped their mother helplessly. 'I'm so sorry, Zoe, they're just excited to see you.'

Bullshit, I thought. The twins were awful because the Normans were such rotten parents. But I had a cunning plan.

Once their mum and dad had gone out, the twins joined me on the sofa. The TV was blaring as usual. The twins were headbutting the sofa cushions and, if I got in the way, headbutting me. I switched off the TV and in the sudden silence, I turned into Kali, the goddess of the severed heads.

'Get off this sofa and sit on the floor! Sit still! I have to tell you something amazing!'

The twins tumbled to the floor, but they were still scrapping. I remained aloof.

'Unless you sit still and listen I will not tell you the Amazing Thing!' I went on, fingers crossed. Eventually they stopped fidgeting and listened.

'If you go to bed now and stay there, quietly, we will be visited by two Amazing Creatures,' I told them. 'But if you don't, I shall phone the creatures now and tell them not to come. You have to be in your beds by the time I count to ten: one, two, three . . .' The twins scrambled to their feet. '. . . four, five, six . . .' They ran upstairs. '. . . seven, eight, nine . . .'

'We in bed!' they shouted. I hoped it wasn't a prediction. I'd suffered from their random urination in the past.

I reached for my phone and called Jess.

'Give it ten minutes,' I told her. 'So far so good.'

Chapter 31

Right on cue, the doorbell rang.

'Don't move!' I warned the twins. 'Stay right there in bed or I'll send them away again!' The twins stayed in their beds, their faces flushed and bright with excitement.

I ran downstairs and opened the door to Jess and Fred: he was carrying a metal box like a toolbox, and she had a rucksack. They had both made up their faces to look like fishes: grey and scaly. I cracked up.

'We just need to slip into our cossies,' whispered Jess.

'OK,' I said. 'And when you're ready, come right on up. The second door on the right.'

I raced back upstairs. The twins were still in their beds. Their eyes were huge – for a moment they looked almost appealing.

'The Amazing Creatures have arrived!' I whispered. 'Not a word! Not a sound! Lie still, or I'll tell them to go away again!'

Soon we heard Jess and Fred coming upstairs, accompanied by fishy watery sounds. They knocked on the twins' door.

'Come in!' I called. Jess and Fred swam into view, their bodies veiled in rippling blue net. They swam up and down the bedroom for a bit, looking fishily from side to side, their mouths glooping open and closed. The twins stared in awe. I had never seen them so quiet.

'Where are we, Sheila?' asked Fred after a while. 'I don't remember this part of the ocean. I told you we should get SpratNav.'

They did a little scene revolving around Fish Wish: all the things fish would like to do if only they had hands.

'If only I had hands!' lamented the Fredfish. 'I'd be able to tie my own shoelaces!'

It was fairly infantile, but the twins laughed their heads off, and Jess and Fred kept it short and sweet as agreed.

'Do it again! Do it again!' yelled the twins as

Jess and Fred took their bow.

'No,' I said firmly. 'That was it. Finished. The end. The Amazing Creatures will come again next time, but only if you both stay in bed now and go to sleep. If I hear one peep out of you from now on, the Amazing Creatures will never come to visit you again and neither will I. OK?'

The twins nodded solemnly.

'OK,' I said. 'Lie down now. Goodnight and sweet dreams.'

The twins lay down and closed their eyes. I couldn't believe it. My plan had worked – so far, anyway.

We tiptoed downstairs and Jess and Fred opened up their toolbox to reveal an amazing collection of stage make-up. They removed their fish faces with cold cream and cotton wool. I congratulated them on a great show.

'I'm so grateful, guys,' I said. 'You have no idea what monsters those kids are usually.'

'We're thinking of doing some shows for schools,' Jess told me. 'So this is great for us – we can try things out.'

'So you really wouldn't mind coming again some-time?'

'No probs!' Jess assured me.

Fred had his back to us, and suddenly he whirled round sporting a grey moustache.

'No talking in the library!' he croaked in a professor's sort of voice.

'This is our pride and joy,' said Jess. 'Stage make-up with loads of beards and moustaches and stuff.'

'God, how amazing!' I raved, admiring the neat rows of facial hair. 'Oh my God! I wish I could play with it!'

'Well, you can if you like,' said Jess. 'We've got to go now, because we promised Mackenzie that we'd drop in on his band rehearsal – it's just up the road. It would be great if we could leave all this stuff here and pick it up on our way back in a couple of hours' time.'

'Of course!' I assured them. 'Oh wow! That would be so cool! Can I really mess around with it and try out some stuff?' I was like a little girl with a dressing-up box.

'Yeah, of course.' Jess showed me how to get the facial hair on and off, and then she and Fred had to leave to meet Mackenzie.

It was still quiet upstairs. I decided not to mess about with the make-up until I was absolutely sure the twins were fast asleep. If they came downstairs and found me sporting a thick red moustache, they would never go back to bed again. I sat and watched a bit of TV with the sound turned down low so I could hear the faintest peep from the twins' bedroom. There was no peep. I waited and waited, and had a cup of coffee. Still silence from upstairs. The fish entertainment had worked a miracle, it seemed.

Suddenly my mobile gave a little buzz. It was a text from Chloe: **AM NEAR THE NORMANS' SO CN I DROP RND & CU?** I replied in the affirmative. I was surprised. Chloe had told me quite sternly many times that she would never re-enter the hellish portals of the twins' house.

I remembered the last time we'd been here together, months ago. I'd been babysitting, obviously, but Chloe had taken up Beast's invitation to go to the sixth form event, even though we weren't sixth formers. He had kind of invited us both, but I hated him back then, and Chloe had had a crush on him, so she'd gone alone. I remembered how she'd turned up here later in the evening, crying her eyes out. She'd been upset because Beast was with another girl at the party or something. It had been a stormy night, and I'd been in the middle of *Wuthering Heights* on DVD. It had been quite gothic.

Then Beast and his sidekicks had arrived, trying to calm her down, and they'd had a shouting match, and they'd woken the twins, and the twins' parents had arrived back early in the middle of the chaos, and . . .

I shuddered at the memory of it and marvelled at how different everything was tonight: silence upstairs, a quiet little text from Chloe – no worries.

Chloe arrived, not broken-hearted, not weeping and not remotely gothic. She gave me a hug.

'I realised I've been a bit mean, leaving you alone with the Norman twins,' she said. 'I've come to give you some support. Have Jess and Fred arrived yet?'

'You liar!' I grinned. 'You've come because you want to see the show. Well, you're too late. It's over, and Fred and Jess have gone. And the twins are fast asleep. So tragically you've missed all the excitement. Come and get a hot chocolate – don't worry, it's the 40-calorie version.'

We went into the kitchen and Chloe looked around, shook her head and sighed.

'God!' she smiled ruefully. 'I'm just remembering last time we were here. I was in such a state, remember? And Beast came round and everything? And the twins peed on everybody from the top of the stairs?'

'Yeah, I was just thinking about that.'

'I was in such a state about Beast!' Chloe shook her head. 'I can't believe the grief I've got myself into over boys. First Beast, then Brendan. Thank God I'm not mad about anybody right now.'

'Not even Dave Cheng?' Dave Cheng is in Beast's rugby team, and we'd seen him in Newquay.

'Oh, ten out of ten for sex appeal,' said Chloe. 'But that's it. I feel so much better right now, don't you? Now I'm not mad about anybody.'

'Definitely,' I said, and meant it. Since I'd had that awful moment delivering leaflets with Matthew, I'd kicked my passion for Beast into touch. OK, I'd been putting in a lot of hours doing those aversion-therapy fantasies about him being unhappily married to Charlie, getting fat and regretful, and following my brilliant career at long range with a nostalgic tear in his eye . . . but it seemed to be working.

The best thing of all was that I'd never told Chloe. She need never know the anguish I'd been putting myself through.

'Boys,' said Chloe, 'are the source of all the angst in the world.'

'True,' I agreed, stirring the chocolate. 'We're better off without them. I'll be entering the convent at the end of next year. As long as the habits are by Vivienne Westwood.'

'What's this box?' asked Chloe, pointing to Jess and Fred's make-up tool kit.

I showed her the neat rows of facial hair and she did that funny little thing I love: she clapped her hands and jumped up and down on the spot.

'Let's try it out!' she yelled. 'That red beard is just right for me!'

Chapter 32

After we'd finished our hot chocs, the transformation began. We took the box upstairs into the master bedroom so we could use Jackie Norman's dressing table. She has a great set of mirrors, but she still always looks a mess. That's kids for you, I suppose.

Chloe chose a red beard and moustache, and found some horn-rimmed glasses.

'I'm a professor from Berlin!' she said, trying to put on an old-fashioned German voice. 'I haf been studying ze sexual behaviour ov tortoises!'

I patted my bristly grey beard and moustache into place, then whitened and roughed up my eyebrows to match.

'I've been living in a cave in Outer Mongolia!' I informed her. 'I'm Zilch the snake charmer.'

'That's not what the snakes tell me!' giggled Chloe. 'They say you're a bit of a pest!'

'I'm going to make myself very, very old,' I decided. I found a hairpiece with a bald effect and tufts of white hair round the crown. Scrunching my hair right back, I pulled the hairpiece on and stared at the weird old guy staring back at me. I pulled a series of ugly faces, all richly comic.

'God, it's so lovely aiming to look hideous instead of trying to be cool and glamorous all the damn time,' I sighed in bliss, adjusting my white sidelong tufts. I found a secret drawer in the make-up box containing warts. I applied three: one to my nose and two to my chin. Chloe was busy blacking out her teeth.

'Yeah,' she agreed. 'Just last week I was dreaming of saving up to have my teeth whitened. But now I realise how wrong you can be: get a load of this.' She grinned enchantingly at me, revealing two big black gaps. 'Black is the new white, yeah?'

I designed pouchy bags under my eyes and crow's-feet lines running right across my cheeks.

'Let's see what Mr Norman can offer in the way of dressing-up togs,' I mused, getting up and opening the built-in wardrobe.

'What time are they due back?' asked Chloe nervously, looking at her watch.

'Don't worry, they said they wouldn't be back before eleven-thirty,' I assured her. 'It's not even nine yet. We've got loads of time.'

I found a pair of men's trousers and put them on. The waist was way too big so I decided to install a massive paunch. The bed was dressed with some cushions so I slipped one down into my knicks. Mr Norman's jacket fitted me quite well – he's not very tall. Chloe chose his sports gear, and dressed herself up in football shorts and shirt.

We stared at ourselves in the full-length mirror: a strange bespectacled red-bearded German prof out jogging, and a fat old scumbag with a bald head, warts and a massive gut.

'At last,' I croaked in a dirty old man voice, 'the makeover of our dreams!' We fell about laughing, and the two old blokes in the mirror were laughing, too.

'You know, Erik,' I said, throwing my arm around Chloe's shoulders, 'I've heard there are two very beautiful girls who live near here. Called Zoe and Chloe.'

'Ja!' agreed Erik. 'Good idea, Zilch. I sink we schould ask zem out.'

'Not girls, goddesses!' I enthused, rubbing my hands in an obscene way. 'Chloe – what a beauty! I love the way she speaks Arabic! Her teeth are so white, they give me a migraine!'

'And Zoe!' cried Prof Erik. 'Not a girl, an angel! So assertif! Ven sche says "No", sche means "No"!'

'And zey are both zo physically fit!' added Zilch, also mysteriously becoming German despite his years in a Mongolian cave. 'I hear zey run thirty miles a day!'

'Ja!' agreed Prof Erik. 'Uphill, too!'

At this point the doorbell rang. We froze.

'It's them!' panicked Chloe. 'They've come back early!'

'They wouldn't ring the doorbell!' My heart was racing in panic. 'They've got their own keys!'

'Unless they've lost them?' breathed Chloe, her eyes wide and terrified behind the horn-rimmed glasses.

We tiptoed out of the Normans' bedroom and looked down the stairs into the hall. We heard voices outside: a boy's voice and a girl's.

'Oh, it'll be Jess and Fred,' I suddenly remembered. 'They've come back to pick up the make-up. Let's show them our glamorous new look! They'll crack up!'

We ran downstairs and flung the door open. But it wasn't Fred and Jess. It was Beast and Charlie.

I felt an electric shock flash through me. I was astounded. Beast couldn't have arrived at a worse moment. What could I say, with my bald head and warts and tufts of ancient hair? And having Charlie there made things a thousand times worse.

Beast and Chloe stared at us in amazement. Then his face broke into a grin. Charlie clapped her hand across her mouth and sniggered, as if she wasn't supposed to laugh.

'Zoe?' said Beast. 'Uhhh, and this must be Chloe? Or is it the famous Dan?'

'Dan had to go,' I said firmly, summoning as much goddess haughtiness as I could muster. 'He couldn't come to terms with my secret identity. It's time you met my alter ego: Zilch the snake charmer.' Beast stared at me and laughed, shook his head in disbelief, and laughed again. He has a lovely, masculine, ringing laugh, but I wished it wasn't directed at me.

'Is this to do with that pantomime you told me about?' asked Charlie, arching her eyebrows in a way which suggested that though our appearance might be amusing, it was also tasteless and weird.

'The pantomime was just a joke,' I said quickly.

'Come in,' said Chloe, disastrously, 'and have a coffee!' I so wanted them to leave immediately and now they had to stay long enough to have a hot drink!

'Thanks, but we can't stay,' said Charlie firmly. 'We're off to celebrate our anniversary.'

A red-hot comet scorched through my intestines. Their anniversary? What was this? A week since they got together, or something?

'Your anniversary?' Luckily Chloe still had some breath left. Mine was gone, as if I'd been punched in the stomach.

'Five years since the founding of Major Events!' announced Charlie.

'Congratulazionz,' I said in my Zilch voice. 'Vor a moment I thought you ver married. But if not, may I haf you vor my seventh wife?' I reached out and stroked Charlie's shoulder. It was the only way I could think of to recover my composure and get back at her.

'Ugh! Cut it out, Zoe!' shrilled Charlie. 'Gross! Pervy!' She shook me off. I was enjoying freaking her out and kept going.

'In my country,' I croaked, 'we haf many wives. I haf six, one for each day ov ze week. You want to be wife number seven? You pretty girl, but too thin!' I grabbed Charlie's arm and squeezed. Beast roared with laughter. Charlie pushed me off.

'Stop it, Zoe, it's weird and disgusting!' she said.

'It's not weird!' grinned Beast. 'It's hilarious!'

'If you marry me,' I said, on a high now and leering hideously into Charlie's face, 'you must put on weight. You must eat goose fat sandwiches vor breakfast and pigs' trotters vor dinner.'

'I'm not going to marry you, you weirdo!' snapped Charlie. She seemed totally unable to enter into the joke. 'Stop being so pervy!'

'Maybe you prefer marry Erik?' I asked Charlie, pulling Chloe forward. 'Erik likes pretty ladies!' Chloe giggled, revealing her blackened teeth.

'Beast, we have to go,' said Charlie, ignoring us and looking at her watch.

'I know, I know,' Beast sighed. 'But I'm enjoying the cabaret.' He pulled an envelope out of his pocket. 'I dropped by,' he said, 'to give you some comps. Your dad told me you were babysitting, and on the way I ran into Charlie, so . . .'

'Amazing coincidence, huh? We decided to have a drink,' said Charlie quickly. 'I love it when things just happen! No planning, just spur of the moment, flash of inspiration – suddenly, wow! You're having the best time!' She looked coyly across at Beast. My mind was whirling. So they hadn't set out together this evening, then – they'd met by accident. If they were an item, wouldn't they have arranged to meet? Wouldn't they have been texting each other non-stop every hour of the day?

Beast opened the envelope, and at the sight of his lovely strong hands my heart missed a beat and all my warts twanged.

'There are half a dozen tickets here,' he said, 'so you can bring your friends – or maybe your wives?' He handed me the envelope. His grey-green eyes were dancing. I opened it and admired the tickets.

'Wunderful!' I croaked, still in character. 'Thank you, sir.'

'One for me!' shrieked Chloe, snatching at the tickets. I shouldered her off.

'So where are you going for your spur-of-the-moment, flash-in-the-pan, best evening ever?' I enquired, abandoning my Zilch voice and giving in to furious jealousy disguised as light-hearted curiosity, with a tasty dash of sarcasm.

'We might go to the Red Lion – that's Beast's favourite place, isn't it, Beastie Boy?' smirked

Charlie. 'They've got a band tonight.'

'Well have fun, you young people,' I croaked, back in character.

'Enjoy your babysitting!' smiled Charlie, managing to make it sound infantile and nerdy. Then she grabbed Beast's arm and turned away, forcing him back down the path. He looked surprised, then kind of exaggerated his surprise as if he was being arrested, then shrugged and shook his head.

'Bye, Zilch! Bye, Erik!' Beast called out. Moments later they disappeared round the corner.

'Wow!' said Chloe as we closed the door. 'Wasn't that hilarious! And I've realised something amazing, really – I'm totally over him. I don't mind if Beast has a girlfriend, and they seemed quite well suited, don't you think?'

There was a mirror on the wall, and for a split second I saw my hideous warty baldness, and imagined Charlie's lovely face alongside it. The contrast was devastating.

Chapter 33

'Oh Gaaaaaaaaaaaaaaahd!' While Beast was on the doorstep, I'd managed to keep my cool, even mess about. Now I let rip: I simply roared. Chloe stared, open-mouthed.

'Zoe? What's wrong?' I marched off to the kitchen, my ears ringing, my heart pounding. I turned on the taps and stood by the kitchen sink, raging, *raging*. I ripped off my moustache. It stung like hell. I pulled off my bald wig and ran my fingers savagely through my hair. I washed my face with soap. It was totally the wrong way to get the make-up off, but I was in a daze. I didn't know what I was doing. Beast had seen me looking *absolutely hideous*. Chloe was peering at me from behind her horn-rimmed professor's glasses.

'I don't think you're supposed to take the make-up off like that, Zoe. Use the cream.'

'I know! I know!' I yelled. I was distraught.

'Zoe?' Chloe stared up at me, totally puzzled. 'What is it?'

'Nothing!' I snarled. I couldn't control myself. I'd thought, for days, that I was over Beast and enjoying my freedom, but suddenly seeing him with Charlie, like this – at a time when I'd never looked more repulsive – had brought all my crazy old feelings back, worse than ever.

'Zoe! Sit down,' said Chloe. She sounded concerned. 'Tell me what's the matter.'

I sat down at the kitchen table, ran my fingers through my hair, and pulled, hard, until the roots stung. There was a silence. Chloe waited. Finally the moment had come to tell her the whole truth.

'You may be over Beast,' I said eventually, in a weird husky voice that seemed to come from outer space, 'and you may not mind if he has a girlfriend, but I . . . I *do* mind. I'm sorry, Chloe, but I mind like hell.' Chloe's eyes widened in amazement.

'What?' she squeaked. 'You mean you –?' I nodded. 'Zoe, this is weird. You've got to take me through this blow-by-blow. I can't get my head round it.'

'What's to tell?' I shrugged helplessly.

'But I thought you hated Beast?'

'No,' I said eventually, and it came out as a massive sigh that seemed to release some long pent-up feeling. 'I don't hate him now. I've realised he's amazing.'

'What made you change your mind?'

'When we were in Newquay and Tam had appendicitis. He knew just what to do. He organised everything. Tam could have died if he hadn't realised she was so ill.'

'And you've felt this way since then?'

'Yes. Basically.'

'But, Zoe, why didn't you tell me?' I squirmed.

'So many reasons. I thought you might still have a little tiny thing about him.'

'But I've told you over and over that I haven't!'

'Well, but . . . you know sometimes we don't tell each other the total truth, because we don't want to hurt each other's feelings.'

'But, Zoe! You must have asked me about this a hundred times!' Chloe sat back in her chair, shaking her head. She took off her horn-rimmed glasses at last, but the beard and moustache were still in place. It gave the conversation a surreal air. 'So that was

283

why you kept on interrogating me about it! Now I understand! Always on and on about how I felt about Beast, every five minutes!'

'Not every five minutes!' I grumbled. 'I just didn't want to tread on your toes, that's all. I wasn't sure what your reaction would be.'

Chloe stared at me for a moment. Her eyes filled with tears. It looked a bit odd, what with the facial hair and everything.

'You really are the best mate,' she said. 'But you don't have to take care of me to that extent, you know. You're the one who needs a bit of support right now.'

'I can cope with it if he's with Charlie,' I said. 'If they're an item, he's welcome to her and he's a bigger idiot than I thought.'

'I've only met her once,' faltered Chloe, 'at the Dolphin Cafe, when he introduced us . . . Don't you like her, then?'

'She's such a show-off,' I said bitterly. 'So up herself it isn't true. But I'm so confused about everything, I don't know if I would feel better about it if she was really nice as well as beautiful . . . Maybe it would be easier to accept.'

'But we don't even know if they are an item.'

'You assumed they were.'

'I was going by the way she was acting. But now I come to think of it, Beast wasn't really like somebody out with his latest squeeze.'

'You're just saying that to make me feel better.'

'No, Zoe, I'm just trying to remember exactly how they were . . . She was going on about Our Anniversary, and it was only Major Events.'

'Which is her uncle's company,' I added.

'Is it?' Chloe pounced on this interesting piece of info. 'Well, poor Beast's in a bit of a fix, then, isn't he? So much harder to say no.'

'Well.' I was recovering my composure now. It was such an immense relief to have told Chloe. And she had reacted brilliantly. 'If he doesn't say no to Charlie because she's the boss's niece, I shall treat him with the contempt he deserves.'

'That's right!' Chloe encouraged me. 'Go girl! Goddesses don't mope about with broken hearts! They soar up on a pillar of fire and turn people into slugs!'

I felt better, and we went upstairs to remove our make-up properly, with cold cream and stuff. I had a very sore lip where I'd ripped off my moustache, and I knew it was still going to be red tomorrow. But my black eye had more or less faded and my beard of scabs was healing fast. There was room in my repertoire for something new and cute.

'What we have to do,' said Chloe firmly, 'is find out what the situation is between Beast and Charlie. Tactfully.'

'And if they are an item,' I declared, 'I will soar up on a pillar of fire and turn her into a . . . what was it?'

'A giant slug.'

'A cockroach.'

'And if they aren't an item, Zoe?' Chloe looked at me in the bathroom mirror, her eyebrows playfully arched. 'Go in there and grab him with both hands!'

A huge tingle ran up my spine at the thought, exploding at the base of my neck. But how could I possibly grab Beast, after he'd seen me all bald and warty? Surely nobody could fancy anyone after seeing them like that?

Chapter 34

The next few days were tense and expectant: Jailhouse Rock was looming now and we were caught up in the final throes. Rumours flew around, especially about Rose Quartz. I devoured the details on the websites and in the magazines.

Rose was wrecked; she was pregnant; she was in love with a hobo; she was going to give up touring; she had seen a vision of Elvis; she had set fire to her own hair in a shopping mall; she had given away all her shoes to charity; she had bought a flock of goats and they wandered free-range through her beach house in Malibu . . . She was even, for a blood-curdling forty-eight hours, in rehab.

I was still delivering flyers with Matthew at the time. As he was in his gap year he spent most of his time at the Major Events office, while I was slaving away at school, so, though relentlessly khaki and nerdy, he always possessed the latest info.

'Beast's tearing his hair out,' he confided, in the middle of the rehab crisis. 'They're trying to line up a substitute act in case Rose drops out, but it's dodgy because if Rose doesn't drop out, they won't need anybody, and it's kind of an insult to say, *"We want you if she's not available, but if she does turn up we won't need you."'*

'God, what a nightmare,' I groaned. 'Is Charlie managing to keep Beast sane?'

'Yeah, of course,' Matthew droned appreciatively. 'Although if I was Beast, I'd be uncontrollable with lust . . .' The terrifying image of Matthew being uncontrollable with lust would remain burned into my memory banks for decades. 'She's totally amazing, right?' He sighed. I didn't bother to agree or, indeed, to inform him that she was, in fact, a Grade-A nitwit.

'She's . . . well, she's a goddess,' breathed Matthew. A spear of molten fire hurtled through my heart. How dare Matthew think Charlie was a goddess? Had he absolutely no judgement? I wasn't going to diss her: it would only look cheap and bitchy, but suddenly it made me wonder about the whole goddess project.

If Charlie was a goddess, I didn't want to be one. The way Matthew had said she was a goddess, accompanied by gross drooling, made me shudder. Suddenly the whole goddess project fell away. The sense of relief was massive: it was like falling upwards and floating away over the clouds. A bit like being a goddess, ironically. But I wasn't: I was just myself again, a slightly overweight schoolgirl with a massive zit on her chin.

Though I had abandoned my attempt to become divine, I still wanted to look the business. Eventually Chloe and I went to pick up our dresses. I'd performed another babysitting miracle with the Normans a few days back, with the help of Jess and Fred's Toddlers' Cabaret, and my finances were now hunky-dory. As long as I didn't see a leper begging in the high street in the next five minutes, the pink dress was as good as mine.

We were on the point of entering the boutique when we bumped into Charlie. She was walking arm in arm with a rather fogeyish young man wearing glasses and a raincoat. Arm in arm didn't mean much with Charlie, though: she'd walked along this same pavement arm in arm with me, for God's sake, when she'd hardly even known me.

'Oh, hi, Zoe!' she grinned. 'And uh – Claire!'

'Chloe,' said Chloe.

'Chloe, yes, sorry. God, my memory! It's hopeless!' She tossed her head back, fluttered her eyelids and tousled her hair about gloriously as if to indicate that only sad losers with nothing going for them were able to remember people's names correctly. 'This is George,' she continued. We said hello. George looked a bit disorientated, possibly because his name was really Gary, but also, possibly, because he was the latest victim of Charlie's intense friendship project and it can be disconcerting.

'Great news, anyway, isn't it, guys?' beamed Charlie.

'What news?' I asked.

'Didn't you know?' She had a way of turning this phrase into a sneer, as if Chloe and I were Neanderthals drooling in a cave somewhere and going slightly extinct. 'Rose is out of rehab and she's arriving tomorrow. I've just put a press release out and now I'm off to the Dolphin Cafe to do an in-depth interview for *The Gazette*.' She smiled adoringly at George. Ah! He was a journalist.

'Keep this under your hat,' she leaned forward with a weird wink, 'but between you and me, I think Beastie Boy only managed to get Rose Quartz on board by pretending to be violently in love with her!'

If Charlie reckoned that was a sensible thing to say in the presence of a journalist, she was clearly even more insane than I had thought. At this point, thank God, she steered George away and we were spared any further ghastliness.

'Great news, then, obviously,' said Chloe, as we turned to enter the boutique. 'Apart from Charlie, who is clearly a maneater of the very highest quality, your only rival appears to be a triple Grammy award-winning legend, whose latest album has sold more than two million copies!'

'Fine, no problem,' I replied. 'With my magic dress on, anything's possible. And if he's not available, who cares? There's always one of the princes.'

'Which one do you fancy?' asked Chloe mischievously.

'I don't care, frankly.' I shrugged. 'I quite fancy an old Italian one with a castle on the Med.'

'It's a bit like Cinderella, isn't it?' giggled Chloe. 'And I'm the ugly sister.'

'You so are not!' I corrected her. 'That's Tam's job.

She's as hideous as they come.'

We tried our dresses on one more time, just to make absolutely sure they were right. Surprisingly, I seemed to have lost quite a bit of weight – and I hadn't even been trying. Pounding the pavements with Matthew may have been agonising at the time, but it seemed to have brought an unexpected benefit. The dress looked more fabulous than ever, because this time it wasn't straining at the seams. Though far from slim, I was no longer lardy: more kind of sleek and curvy.

'Wait till Beast sees you in this!' whispered Chloe. 'It'll knock his socks off!' I stared at my reflection. 'You look like a movie star!'

I knew I didn't look like a movie star, but I did at least look my very best. This dress was magic. The cut of it was just somehow outrageously flattering. I couldn't believe what a difference the right clothes could make. I had a feeling that the dress was a bit like a suit of armour: it made me feel kind of defended and safe. I was in danger of becoming ludicrously, superstitiously attached to a garment.

As for Chloe, she had been transformed by her simple little black number. Her hair glowed like fire, her white skin was flawless and her green eyes sparkled.

'Well, you look like you have always been meant to look,' I beamed. Chloe turned round and looked at her own back view. 'Fabulous!'

'It's funny, I think I do quite like black after all,' she mused. I breathed a huge sigh of relief. I had been trying to get Chloe to see the point of black for months, but somehow it had happened all by itself. However, I would be kind of sad and disappointed if she never wore anything adorned with orange tortoises ever again. It's funny how life surprises you: your feelings change in unexpected ways, and suddenly you feel liberated from ideas that have been dragging you down for ages.

I felt a bit like that about Beast, now. Somehow, when I was wearing the magic dress I didn't feel that anything could hurt me: I could face anything, even the sight of Beast and Charlie in a clinch. I had, in some mysterious way, finally made it to a restful mountaintop.

Chapter 35

Finally the great day dawned. The leaflets were all distributed, the tickets were sold out, and Rose Quartz's little spell in rehab had done wonders for our coverage. Even the national newspapers had got excited about the possibility of Jailhouse Rock being cancelled because Rose was having a crisis.

As I was applying my lipstick (Hot Finale), a dog barked from my handbag. I was going to have to replace that ringtone with something more classy – a pack of wolves maybe. Chloe and I had been texting each other for the past half hour, exchanging exciting details of our preparations. Chloe had dropped her mascara down the loo, and I had been freaked out by a spider running across the bathroom mirror. Were these omens, signs that the universe was against us?

I grabbed my phone, eager for her latest disaster. But it was a text from Beast. My heart gave a demented little skip, even though I had told it sternly that as an organism we were not, now, interested in Mr Hawkins. I hadn't seen him since the painfully ludicrous evening when he'd come round to the Normans and I'd cringed behind the front door, dressed as a hideous peasant with warts and a beard.

ZOE COME BACKSTAGE AT ABOUT 7 IF YOU WANT TO MEET ROSE. BRING CHLOE TOO. SEE YOU THEN.

Wow! I had never in my wildest dreams imagined I'd actually get to *meet* Rose. My heart now gave several huge demented lurches, with my blessing. Anxiously I glanced at myself in the mirror. The pink dress did it for me: I had to admit it looked fabulous, so though, of course, I would be paralysed with embarrassment when I met Rose, at least I would look OK. I wondered what she would be wearing – something amazing, no doubt, because she is famous for her dazzling wardrobe.

I called Chloe right away to tell her we'd been selected to meet the goddess.

'Aw naaaaow!' she literally screamed in my ear. 'I don't belieeeeeve it!'

We agreed to meet at the stage door in half an hour and made a pact that if either of us fainted or puked with excitement when being introduced to Rose, the other would join in.

Dad gave me a lift there. 'Well, you look tickety-boo, old boy,' he admitted as I climbed out of the car. 'Enjoy it. And if the creature Rose offers you any recreational drugs . . .'

'I'll bring some home for you in a doggy bag, obviously, Dad!' I quipped sardonically. I gave him a long hard look to convince him of my essential good sense and sanity, slammed the car door and teetered off in my killer heels.

Chloe was waiting and we launched ourselves into a hysterical hug, whilst, of course, ensuring that we didn't smudge our make-up or crease our dresses.

'You really do look like a goddess!' breathed Chloe.

'No, no, Chloe! That goddess thing is so last century!' I purred. 'Have I managed to look human? That's what I'm worried about.'

'That dress, though!' Chloe gazed at me in admiration. 'It's awesome!'

'Yeah, and so is yours! Move over, Cate Blanchett! Anyway, enough of us, let's get in there! Oh God!

I hope I don't spit in her face by accident when we're introduced!'

'I hope she spits in my face!' whispered Chloe. 'Then we could collect the spit and sell it on eBay!'

There was a man who looked slightly like a meerkat in a little office by the stage door. He squinted at us through a window.

'Zoe and Chloe!' I told him. 'Harry Hawkins told us to come to the stage door at seven.' The meerkat consulted some notes, then made a phone call.

'OK, he'll be down in a minute,' he told us. We waited in hysterical excitement. My pulse was thrashing and my heart was beating so hard, my whole body had become a samba band. It was handy being so nervous about meeting Rose, because I couldn't really tell if I was nervous about seeing Beast again or not.

Moments later Beast appeared looking pale and hectic. My heart performed a couple of somersaults for old times' sake. His hair was tousled, as if he'd been tearing it. I hoped it wasn't because Charlie or Rose had been running their fingers through it. Although I was definitely over Beast now, I still seemed to be jealous. For a split second he looked right into my eyes and his smile somehow zipped right down the backs of my legs, setting them on fire. I was going to have to give my body a stern talking-to, later.

'Zoe, Chloe, great to see you, come this way,' he said, beckoning. We followed him through a maze of corridors. Loads of people were bustling about: guys in headphones carrying clipboards, random muscular types wearing stained T-shirts, and they all greeted Beast as we passed. I felt proud just to be a hanger-on.

'OK, let me fill you in on the situation,' said Beast, pausing in a quiet corner. 'Rose is fine, but her minder has got flu and Rose has had a row with her manager and she won't speak to anyone from that office. Charlie was with her for a while, but you know Charlie . . .' He hesitated, and shook his head in a way that was not as affectionate as I would have expected. '. . . she managed to get up her nose, big time, so Rose threw her out.' Though horrified at the news that the goddesses had been involved in a cat-fight, I only hoped it had been captured on CCTV so eventually we'd all be able to watch it on YouTube.

'Rose is rattled,' Beast went on. 'She needs a bit of company: she's always nervous before she goes on. So

I want you to stay with her and be very, very soothing and supportive, OK?'

Beast look nervously to the right and then to the left, and dropped his voice. 'Make sure she has everything she wants. And don't let her do anything stupid.' He ran his fingers through his hair and looked at us with a wild expression not a million miles from panic.

We nodded, speechless with terror. He led us around a corner to the dressing rooms and knocked on a door. There was a faint reply, and he opened the door and led us in. I saw heaps of clothes everywhere, lights, mirrors, and somebody sitting at a dressing table. I don't think my heart has ever beat so fast without lurve being involved.

'Rose,' he said, 'this is Zoe and Chloe, my two best girls. They'll keep you company and get you anything you want.'

Rose turned around in her chair, the light of the dozen bulbs round the mirror throwing her face into relief.

'My freakin' eyebrows!' she yelled. 'Kate usually does my eyebrows! I look like a heap of shit!'

'Maybe Zoe can help you,' said Beast, looking frazzled. 'She's the queen of eyebrows.' I was startled to receive this sudden title, but willing to do anything to help poor Beast.

'Excuse me for a bit,' he said, backing towards the door, 'I've got stuff to do.'

Rose Quartz fixed me with a pleading stare. 'Can you do eyebrows?' she demanded. 'You, the one in the pink dress. Can you do eyebrows? I can't go on looking like this, this is terrible. Sorry, I'm always hyper before a gig. I can't stop talking. What was your name again?' I approached her, trying not to be overawed because I knew the best thing would be to treat her just as if she was one of our mates.

'I'm Zoe, this is Chloe,' I said. 'Sure, I'll have a go if you like.'

'Great! Be my guest! But don't breathe in my face!'

'I won't breathe at all,' I promised her.

'And you – uh, sorry, Chloe – can you go and get me a hot dog with onions and ketchup and mustard? And a coke?'

'Diet Coke or regular?' asked Chloe nervously. I thought this showed tremendous presence of mind.

'Regular, regular,' said Rose. 'Caffeine addiction. Ha ha! It wasn't that, by the way. It was only pre-scription painkillers. Don't believe anything you read in those damn magazines. Knock five times when you come back.'

'OK,' Chloe said, and disappeared.

'Look at my eyebrows,' commanded Rose. 'The right one's a disaster!' I inspected her eyebrows.

'I suggest we start again,' I said, trying to sound calm even though I was shaking in my shoes at the thought that I was standing right next to Rose Quartz – indeed, about to mess with her face! I was close enough to touch the legendary snake tattoo on her right shoulder, although I couldn't actually see it because she was wearing a kind of towel all over her top half to protect her dress – a bit like those cloths guys wear in old movies when they go to get a shave at the barber.

Rose Quartz looked up at me. I was surprised at how ordinary she looked, up close and personal and without much make-up on. She's not really famous for her beauty, it's her gravelly voice and the way she belts out songs. And her legs, of course. She'd shaved her head about six weeks ago, not out of some kind of mad impulse, but because her auntie had been diagnosed with cancer and she'd had to have chemo and was losing her hair, so Rose did it to show solidarity. For this reason alone I respected her big time. Plus it meant she wouldn't get all stressy about her hair: it was just a kind of stubble of blonde bristles all over, and I have to say it looked fabulous.

'Get on with it.' Rose threw down her eyebrow pencil. 'There's remover stuff and everything . . .' She lifted her face towards me and looked piercingly at me for a moment. 'Amazing dress,' she murmured, and reached out and stroked my thigh. For a split second I had a moment of sheer terror that she was hitting on me. 'Satin,' she murmured, 'divine.'

Then she folded her hands in her lap and closed her eyes. I kicked off my killer heels and grabbed a wad of cotton wool.

'Where did you get it?' asked Rose.

'A little local boutique,' I stammered.

'Always the best,' said Rose. 'Start again with the eyebrows. I know they're a disaster.'

Gently I removed Rose's previous attempt at eyebrows, thanking my lucky stars that I'd done eyebrows for my friends so many times. Especially Chloe.

'That goddam Kate,' grumbled Rose, her eyes still closed. 'I'm going to sack her! Flu, for God's sake. I mean, duh! Today of all days! I told her to go and get an anti-flu shot! I had one. I mean, you can't let people down, especially charity! What charity is it again?'

'Amnesty,' I said, hoping my fingers would stop trembling soon as it was a bit of a challenge to redesign a diva's eyebrows with your digits vibrating for England.

'Poor prisoners,' sighed Rose. 'I so love 'em. I wish I could let 'em all out right now! I'd hate to be in prison, I couldn't handle it for five minutes, I'd freak out big time and be screaming and climbing the walls. I can't bear to be shut in.'

I glanced anxiously around the dressing room, hoping she wasn't going to start any of that screaming and wall-climbing right now.

'I hope your friend hurries up,' said Rose. 'I'm absolutely starving.'

Ten minutes later I had got the eyebrows right. I knew exactly how they should look because there's a photo of Rose Quartz in the music montage on my bedroom wall. I had managed to do it without breathing in her face, and my fingers had stopped trembling. Then there were five knocks on the door, and Rose opened her eyes.

'Come in!' she shouted. A blast of nicotine hit my face. I vowed never, ever to smoke. Rose peered fiercely at her reflection. 'Well done – jackpot – thanks so much!' She nodded. Thank God she approved of the eyebrows. 'I have to get up and have this hot dog now,' said Rose. I stood back as she got up and flung aside her towel. She was wearing an amazing white dress.

Chloe had re-entered, accompanied by a delicious smell. Rose surveyed herself again in the full-length mirror, paying special attention to her eyebrows.

'You've done a great job,' she told me. 'In a minute you must do my eyes.'

Chloe stood there looking embarrassed and holding the tray. Rose made a space for it on the dressing table, pushing a heap of make-up and under-wear out of the way, then sat down again and beamed delightedly at the hot dog.

'Great. Thanks. Now nobody talk to me for five minutes because I have to eat in silence.'

We nodded and backed off to give her space. She seemed happily oblivious of us, now, plugging in her iPod and jiggling about as she picked up the hot dog. She took a bite and munched away contentedly. Chloe and I watched in fascination from our place by the back wall. The dressing room was a tip. The floor was covered with debris: tissues, shoes, tights, food wrappers, empty cigarette cartons.

Everywhere there was a strong spicy fragrance: I would have to ask her what perfume she used, although I doubted if I would be able to afford it.

Rose took another bite of her hot dog . . . and a huge dollop of fried onions, liberally garnished with mustard and ketchup, leapt out of the side of the roll and splatted down on to her lap!

'Aw naaaaaow!' Rose shrieked. She threw the hot dog aside – it knocked into the plastic cup of coke, which tipped over, flooding the dressing table and splashing her dress. She jumped to her feet, swearing and hopping about in fury.

'Look at this! Look at this!' she screamed. Her lovely white dress was totally trashed: a huge stain of mustard and ketchup and grease was smeared right across the front of her skirt, and the rest of the dress was horribly spattered with coke stains. 'Get Harry! Get Harry!' she screamed. 'This is a disaster.' She was jumping up and down. 'Get Harry!' I whipped out my phone and rang Beast's number. 'That goddam Kate! My whole wardrobe is with her! This is my only dress! I can't go on! I'll sack her! I'll sack the whole goddam pack of them!' She flew into the bathroom. We heard the taps turned on, and another cascade of swearing.

'Yes?' Beast answered in my ear.

'You'd better come and see Rose,' I told him. 'I hate to have to tell you this, but there's been a bit of a disaster.'

Chapter 36

Beast arrived, looking apprehensive. Rose confronted him, gesturing at her stained dress.

'Look!' she screamed. 'Look what just happened! This is the only dress I have with me, due to the fact that I'm surrounded by idiots and my tour wardrobe is in freakin' Paris!! Do something, Harry!'

Beast shrugged and looked tense. 'The shops are all shut . . .' He started tugging at his hair.

'Harry! I am literally not going on unless you can find me something fabulous!' Beast's eyes were wild: he looked helplessly at me, at Chloe, then back at Rose. Suddenly I had an idea. In a way it was a terrible idea, because it meant my evening had to end right here and now. But it was a possible way out of this nightmare – possibly the only way out.

'Er, Rose?' I asked. 'You said you liked this dress . . .'
Rose looked at me and her gaze changed.

'Yes! My God! You're about my size, too!' Her face changed from anguish to hope.

'You'd be welcome to try it,' I suggested. 'It's nothing much, but . . .'

'No . . . no . . .' Rose approached me like a snake slithering towards a helpless mouse. 'Can I really try it? Would you mind?'

'I'll leave you to it, then,' said Beast hastily, and he went out, only pausing at the door to give me a very strange look: of pleading, desperation and, unless I'm very much mistaken, lifelong gratitude.

I pulled off the dress and Rose dived into it. Of course, she looked fabulous. She preened herself in the mirror and did a few manoeuvres.

'It's OK, it's OK,' she said excitedly. 'Do you mind, Zoe? I'm really grateful. You can have it back afterwards . . . I always travel in my grey jog pants.'

'It's fine,' I said. 'Go ahead. It's an honour!'

'OK then,' said Rose briskly. 'We're in business. There's a bathrobe in the shower room – help yourself.'

When she left the dressing room to do her set, I insisted that Chloe should go out and watch her sing, but, of course, being in bra and pants and wrapped in a big white towelling robe, I had to stay where I was. It was like those horrible dreams you have sometimes, when you're out in public and have mysteriously forgotten to get dressed.

I sat down to listen to Rose's appearance on stage over the PA system. I heard her being introduced and the huge wave of cheering as the massive audience welcomed her. Her band launched into their first number: *Let It Go*. She was giving it everything. What a star!

And despite being a bit stressed out and diva-ish, she'd been quite nice to us. If only I could see her now, with my dress enjoying its finest hour – on the back of a real goddess – divine clothing for a divine performer. It had been a thrill to be with her and help her get ready, though. Something to tell the grandchildren – if I ever had any.

There was a knock on the door.

'Zoe!' It was Beast's voice. I jumped up, agitated. He mustn't see me like this! My heart lurched into overdrive.

'Just a minute!' I yelled. 'I'm not decent!' I pulled the robe more tightly around me and ran to the door.

'Zoe! Don't you want to come and watch Rose

doing her set? Come on, don't be shy!'

'Harry,' I said, using his name for the very first time (I don't know why), 'listen. I'm just wrapped in a towel here. I look grotesque!'

'Don't be stupid, Zoe,' said Beast patiently. 'I've got some clothes for you anyway. Open the door!' I hesitated in a boiling silence, tongue-tied, my pulse racing. 'Let me in!' Beast went on. 'Or I'll break the freakin' door down!'

Cringing in my towelling robe, I turned the lock, Beast stepped in and the door slammed shut behind him. He stood there looking magnificent. All the stress and angst had gone from his face – he looked taller and his eyes were dazzling.

'Here you are . . .' He brandished a sports bag. 'Lizzie at the merch stand said you could borrow these. They're not exactly Gucci, but who cares? You always look beautiful to me whatever you're wearing.' He thought I looked beautiful? A huge blush exploded across my face and I stared at him in disbelief.

'I realised I was still crazy about you when I saw you dressed up as a little old man!' said Beast. His voice was husky and he was trembling. 'It was the warts and the baldness that did it for me.' He laughed nervously. I uttered a strange hysterical squeak, and clapped my hand across my mouth.

'I know you told me to get lost once, and you can tell me to again if you like,' he said. 'But Chloe promised me you wouldn't be so harsh this time.'

'Chloe promised . . . ?'

'I saw her just now, backstage,' said Beast. 'She told me you might not mind if I asked you out again . . . ?'

For some crazy reason, I burst into tears. Beast dropped the stuff he was carrying and swept me up into his arms. He squeezed every breath out of my body. My poor little heart pounded away like mad, and through the white fluffy towelling robe, I could feel his heart thumping, too.

'What . . .' I asked feebly, when I got my breath back '. . . what about Charlie?'

'Charlie was never even on my radar,' he said, his breath hot on my hair. 'She's a fantasist. It was always you I wanted.' Then he kissed my ear. He kissed one of my horrible weird ears! He must really like me, then. I gave myself up to a delirious moment of sheer melting bliss, whilst Rose continued belting out *Let It Go*.

'The last few weeks have been really tough,' whispered Beast. 'I thought you still hated me.'

'Well, I do, of course,' I croaked, clinging on for dear life.

'I didn't know . . .' said Beast '. . . what you were thinking . . . what was going on . . .'

'I didn't know, either,' I murmured, the lovely citrus smell of his skin washing over me.

'I've changed,' Beast went on, 'since you ripped into me that time and told me how revolting I was. You were right. I was an animal.'

'A beast,' I agreed. 'But please don't change into a naff prince in tights. That would be gross.'

'I promise,' whispered Beast. 'And you'd better not change one tiny detail, either. I like you as you are: warts and all.' Nigel throbbed in ecstasy. I think he was a little bit in love with Beast, too.

We sank into a kiss which lasted about ten thousand years, and caused all the bamboo forests in China to bloom. Then Rose's song finished and there was a storm of applause. Our kiss ended.

Beast looked up at the PA system. 'Seems as if the audience enjoyed that as much as we did.' He grinned. 'Look, much as I'd like to spend the next five days standing here like this, we have to see Rose's set. Here . . .' He reached down into the sports bag and offered me the stuff he'd brought: a big Jailhouse Rock sweatshirt and a pair of footless tights. I took them into the bathroom and dived into them, then emerged and put on my killer heels.

'Beautiful!' said Beast with a grin. 'Come on, we can watch Rose from backstage!'

He led me through another maze of corridors and then into a dark area at the side of the stage. We had a great view of Rose strutting her stuff in my pink dress. Beast stood behind me with his arms wrapped round me. I could feel his breath on my hair and neck. I couldn't believe it, after all my weeks of anguish: here I was being hugged by Beast, something I'd decided was never going to happen.

'She looks great in my dress!' I yelled.

'You really got me out of jail tonight, babe!' roared Beast. 'Giving her the dress off your back! You're a legend!'

'Well, Rose is a goddess!' I shouted.

'Just an ordinary goddess, though!' he roared in my ear. 'She can't compete with the one and only Zoe Morris!' And he gave me such a squeeze, all the breath in my body shot out of my mouth in an unattractive bark. Luckily the music was so loud, nobody heard.

Suddenly I caught sight of Chloe across the stage, watching from the wings opposite. Our eyes met and she grinned in delight, giving me the thumbs up. Rose finished her number and the whole place shook in another eruption of cheering.

'OK!' screamed Rose. 'Let's hear it for all our brothers and sisters in jail for their beliefs! Justice for them! Freedom!'

I realised that I had somehow got out of a private jail of my own. At last, wrapped in my Jailhouse Rock sweatshirt, wrapped in my Beast, with my hair all over the place and my make-up smudged by his shoulder, I actually felt like a goddess. It was nothing to do with hair or clothes or fitness or any of that, it was just the kind of divine moment that could happen in anybody's life, and I sent out a silent *thank you* to the big, black, mysterious, echoing universe.

Turn over for a taster of

Girl, 15: Flirting for England

by Sue Limb

Join Jess Jordan in a tale of Gallic passion,
muddy tents and aggressive cows!

'Limb's heroine is cleverer than Rennison's, less bonkers
than McKay's, but just as captivating'
The Times

Dear Ed

My dear Edouard

Darling Ed!

Dear Edouard,

    . . . or may I call you Ed? Edouard is so . . . it sounds a bit . . .

Oh, no! Insulting him already! Being rude about his name! Jess screwed up the piece of paper and threw it at the bin. It missed.

Dear Edouard,

    You're my French exchange partner . . .

He knows that already, retardo! Jess screwed up the piece of paper and threw it at the bin. It missed.

Dear Edouard,

  Hi! My name's Jess Jordan and apparently we're exchange partners . . .

'Apparently'? As if it had all happened by accident and Jess was a bit embarrassed about it? And would, to be honest, have preferred to exchange with a monkey?

Jess screwed up the piece of paper and also screwed up her eyes, her fists and her toes, and uttered a strangled cry of anguish. Why was this so damn difficult? She looked out of the window. It was raining. Mustn't mention that. French people probably thought it rained in England all the time.

If only she hadn't got herself into this mess. A couple of weeks ago, the French teacher Mrs Bailey had said she had 'an announcement to make about the forthcoming French exchange scheme'. She'd looked awkward.

'Things are a bit unusual this year,' she'd said, 'because there are more French boys wanting to take part than English boys. So I'm afraid some of you girls will have to have a French boy as your exchange partner. Put your hand up if you don't mind.'

Jess's arm had shot up so fast, she'd almost dislocated her shoulder. A French boy! What could be more sexy? Jess was dazzled by the thought of all those French footballers with their shiny brown eyes and pouty French lips.

But now, trying to write her first letter to the guy, she was *so* wishing she hadn't. If only Edouard had been a girl, Jess could easily have dashed off a letter introducing herself, no problem. But now she felt self-conscious. She had to come across as attractive, charismatic and mysterious, even if her country *was* saturated with rain.

Dear Edouard,

I'm your French exchange partner. I'm sorry I have to write in English, as my French is totally useless. My name's Jess Jordan and I live in a loft-style apartment overlooking twinkling skyscrapers. My mum is descended from the Royal House of Portugal. Her name is Joanna the Slightly Mad. My dad lives in Hollywood. He's a film producer. I was born on a stormy night in July, when it rained rubies . . .

Girl, 15: Flirting for England
AVAILABLE NOW